BOUND

ISABELLE TAYLOR

KDP Paperback ISBN: 979-8-285090-83-0

IngramSpark Paperback ISBN: 978-1-067061-72-2

IngramSpark Hardcover ISBN: 978-1-067061-73-9

CONTENT WARNINGS

Ritualistic sex, size kink, brief depictions of painful sex, cockwarming, knotting, He Wants To Eat Her But He (Mostly) Gets Over It, age gap, loss of virginity.

ONE

"You can do this," Ruby consoled herself as she looked up at the forest on the edge of town. "It's a simple spell. Everything that comes next..."

She trailed off, gripping her ritual dagger tightly. She had been trying not to think about what happened after she opened that portal to the Bygone's void. It was much easier to think about the town behind her.

"Everything that happens next is for Sweetsguard," she reminded herself.

She took a step toward the forest.

A voice rang out behind her, loud and annoying.

"Don't pretend you're doing this for us," called Glenda Rivershore, standing at her clothesline with a washing basket perched on her wide hip. "You want to get yourself killed for your own dumb glory, you go right ahead. But don't pretend you're being *noble*."

Ruby pocketed her dagger and turned. "I'm just trying to renew the ward, Glenda. *Somebody* has to."

"And our local witch is rushing to the rescue," Glenda drawled, snapping a sheet with such force it hurt Ruby's ears. "You know what's going to happen when you step into a Skullstalker's void, let alone into You-Know-Who's void? That bony bastard is going to *eat* you. Or, at the very least, steal you away like he does to any traveler dumb enough to step off the path in those woods!"

Ruby desperately wanted to tell her that if she got eaten, at least she wouldn't have to put up with Glenda's constant insults. Or the townsfolk turning their noses up at her for living alone at the edge of town, studying magic, and praying to Paimon, the goat deity who protected the town. Witches were revered, to be sure. But they weren't smiled at on market day.

"Somebody has to risk it," she reminded Glenda. "Paimon has stopped answering. We need *someone* to renew his ward."

Glenda snorted, shuffling a sheet onto the line. "You mean your beloved magic is dying, and you're *terrified* of being just like us regular folk. I *know* witches, little girl. They all think they're so much better than us. So, if you want to go and give yourself to that thing, go right ahead."

Her door slammed open. Three children spilled out, chasing each other and singing a song Ruby herself had sung when she was young: *"Keep to the light and be wary, keep to the map and don't stray. Keep to the path and hurry along, or the Bygone will steal you away. Into his void of darkness deep, to wander and cry and never sleep—*"

"Children," Glenda snapped. "Don't say You-Know-Who's name out loud! And wave goodbye to the witch. We'll have to get a new one after this."

"Bye, witch," the children chorused.

Ruby sighed and waved at them as they ran toward the middle of town. She had been born in Sweetsguard, and one day, she would like to be buried here. But there were times when she wondered if there wasn't somewhere that appreciated her talents as a witch instead of using her services and leaving with a suspicious huff.

Not that it mattered now. There was no place like that where she was headed—only darkness and danger and, hopefully, a solution. If the ward failed, demons would pour into their town and devour everything in their path.

Ruby wasn't about to let that happen, even if nobody thanked her for fixing it.

"If I don't come back," she called to Glenda, "You *will* have to send for a new witch."

"Yes, yes." Glenda waved her peg basket at her. "Away with you."

Ruby sighed and paused for one last look. If she squinted, she could see the town square, washed with morning light: bakers placing bread in windows, milkmaids lugging milk pails, stall owners setting up their wares. Everybody called good morning as they passed, full of cheer they never shared with her. Even so, she was full of fondness for it. The ramshackle stores had never looked so beautiful, and the children's laughter had never sounded so sweet.

And in the middle of it all, Paimon's ward. The great big slab had been set up so many generations ago that the origin was lost to time. But for all that time, it had been glossy and strong, the magic so vivid she could feel it thrumming when she placed her hand on it.

Not anymore. The goat horn rune was fading. The stone was drying and chipping. Soon, it would crack entirely—unless Ruby found someone to renew it. And if Paimon wasn't answering, she would have to seek help elsewhere.

Even if it meant venturing into Skullstalker voids. Into the *Bygone's* void, where wandering souls never found peace. And offering herself up to be eaten.

Skullstalkers were well known for eating humans, after all. It would be preferable to the fate the stories promised: endless wandering through the dark.

Ruby shuddered and took her first step into the woods.

"Hope You-Know-Who eats you fast," Glenda called.

It was possibly the nicest thing Glenda had ever said to her.

"Thanks," Ruby called back grudgingly.

She tightened her cloak. Then she stepped forward and let the woods swallow her up.

Forests were supposed to be full of birdsong and animals chittering. Silence meant you had stumbled somewhere the veil was thin. If you were unlucky, you would wander into a void—the dimensions bordering the mortal realm, filled with demons and spirits and, worst of all, Skullstalkers.

Skullstalkers like the Bygone.

Ruby slid her dagger out of her pocket. It was well-kept and shiny, just like it had been when the last witch of Sweetsguard had given it to her. Ruby polished it every morning before breakfast.

"Okay," she murmured, pressing the dagger tip against her palm. "Let's begin. Paimon, protect me."

It was probably useless to evoke his name now. But she had been a devoted follower of the local goat deity her whole life. Despite his silence and her fading magic, she couldn't stop hoping he still heard her.

She sliced a red thatch through her lifeline.

"*Open the way,*" she whispered, her voice vibrating through the trees in an otherworldly echo. "*Charter me to the Skullstalker void of lost souls, where all wander endlessly. Show me the Bygone.*"

Her magic was weak. A small, thin circle appeared in the air, slow and struggling. It was already trying to close and hadn't even opened properly.

"Come on," she gritted. "*Please.*"

She reached out. Her bloody palm touched the circle.

Blue light exploded through the forest. Ruby stumbled back with a gasp. Blue light glimmered in her hair before fading, leaving only the sparks thrown by the wheeling circle in front of her.

For a moment, it had almost been like when Paimon

was around. No, that wasn't right—for a moment, she'd felt more power than Paimon ever gave her. But that feeling was fading, and time was running out.

Ruby braced herself. She couldn't see the horrors that waited, but she could see darkness: heavy and swarming. Black tendrils reached out of the portal to brush her cheek.

She shivered. Then she stepped into the dark.

The forest vanished, and the burning blue portal vanished with it. For a second, there was only darkness. It was light and airy, trailing over her skin and snaking around her neck.

Ruby let out a terrified noise. She was going to get eaten before she even got to talk to the Bygone!

Then, the darkness relented. Ruby opened her eyes.

She was standing in the middle of a shrouded forest. Skeletal trees protruded from the earth, shadows dripping off the leaves.

Ruby shuddered. It looked like an enchanted forest from a fairy tale—one you were never supposed to enter.

There were no doomed souls. Ruby had been expecting at least a few. All the stories involved damned souls who had been wandering so long they forgot who they were.

Something barked beside her. Ruby startled, swinging her knife toward the sound.

"Don't eat me yet," she yelled. Then she stopped.

A dog spirit sat contentedly among the shadowy

leaves. It was large and shabby and mostly transparent, its big tail wagging as it cocked its head at her. If it was corporeal, its fur would probably be snow-white.

"Oh," Ruby said, sagging with relief. She held out a hand cautiously, trying to remember any warnings about dog spirits. But the dog didn't *look* like a secret demon. It trotted up to her and licked her hand.

Ruby laughed, amazed. Its tongue felt like the lightest feather against her palm.

"And hello to you too," she said warmly. "Don't tell me he stole *you*. My day's already going terribly; I couldn't stand adding another tragedy on top of it."

The dog woofed quietly, its tail thumping harder.

Ruby watched its happy stature. The forest surrounding them seemed like a miserable place for a spirit to spend its time, but it seemed content enough.

"Well," she said, scratching its ghostly scruff. "You seem okay. Even if you did get—"

A low, dangerous voice spoke up behind her.

"I warned you what would happen if you woke me again," it growled.

Cold fear trickled down Ruby's spine. There was an otherworldly quality behind the words, not unlike when she had been reciting the portal spell. There was no one else it could belong to except...

She turned, clutching her dagger tightly to her chest as she came face to face with the Bygone.

The Skullstalker was so tall he blotted out the meager evening light. He was dressed in nothing but a dark loin-cloth, and his skin was an unnatural shade of blue, except for his arms, which swarmed with darkness down to his fingertips. His black hands were tipped with sharp claws, and a black panther tail lashed behind him.

A skull mask covered the top half of his face. White ram horns curled out the top of it. Shadows leaked out from behind the mask, betraying its monstrous nature. The skull's eye sockets were huge, exposing giant, gleaming black eyes with specks of blue shimmering in the middle, fixed on her with an intensity that made her think of a wolf eyeing his prey.

"You are not the dog spirit," the Bygone continued, his voice full of scraping rocks.

Ruby shuddered. She always hoped she would die an old woman in bed. She didn't think she would have to look her death in the face.

"Mortal," he said, his fangs glinting. "Why do you disturb my slumber?"

Ruby wet her lips. Her throat was suddenly bone-dry.

"I," she said. "I didn't mean…"

Her gaze fell on something behind him. At first, she thought it was just a mass of sticks. Then she squinted and noticed the fur lining the sides, shadowy feathers tucked in between the twigs.

A nest, Ruby realized with a shudder. *I woke a Skull-stalker from its nest.*

It was the first thing she had learned when the previous witch trained her on dealing with wild animals. Never approach their nest. And never—*ever*—wake them. Not that a Skullstalker was an animal. Ruby would take any wolf or lion or even a rabid basilisk over a Skull-stalker.

"I'm sorry," she said, stumbling over her words. "If you just... give me a second to explain..."

The Bygone cocked its head. *Sizing up its prey,* Ruby thought in a panic.

She checked behind her to make sure the dog spirit was safe and sagged with relief when she saw nothing but the forest. It was now or never.

She brought her dagger to her palm, slashing a second cut over her lifeline. The cuts formed a cross, one of the last things the previous witch of Sweetsguard had taught her before she passed.

Crosses are for binding, the witch had said. *I pray you never need this spell. But if you do... cast with all your heart.*

That was one thing Ruby was always good at. She was incapable of doing anything without putting her whole heart into it. She hoped it would work in her favor today.

"*Chain us until it is fulfilled,*" she rasped.

The cross on her hand glowed. Slick chains rushed from the wound, circling them both before vanishing in a shower of pink mist.

The Bygone raised a hand to examine her blood on his fingers No, not his fingers—his claws, Ruby realized with mounting fear. For all he stood on two legs and spoke the mortal tongue, he was still a beast.

"You bound me," said the Bygone, surprised.

"I bound *us,*" she corrected. She lifted her chin,

hoping he didn't notice how hard she was shaking. She was a powerful witch, but she had never traveled far from her small town. She felt nowhere near prepared to face a Skullstalker, especially the one that was evoked when you wanted your children to behave.

"You can do..." Ruby shivered. "Whatever you wish with me. But first, you must grant me a boon."

He cocked his head at her again. Less prey this time, more curiosity. He looked almost bored, like he would rather be back in his nest.

"Alright, little witch," he said, his voice dangerously soft. "What do you wish of me? Power? Riches?"

"The protection ward in my town is failing," Ruby blurted. "Our local deity, Paimon... he isn't answering, and time is running out. We need someone to renew the ward."

The Bygone blinked. His black eyes were so much larger than a human's. Every time Ruby looked at them, they seemed to get bigger.

"Paimon," the Bygone repeated. "Hmm."

He looked away, his hand curling at his side. For a moment, his claws retracted, and Ruby startled. She didn't know he could do that.

Then the Bygone cracked its neck and looked at her again. "I will do this."

"Thank you," Ruby breathed. Relief and horror surged through her all at once. The deal was sealed, and she could feel the magic knitting the promise into existence. There was only one thing left to do.

"I'm ready," she declared.

She closed her eyes and waited. Shadows drifted up from rotting leaves and curled sickeningly around her ankles. Strange, unfamiliar birdsong trilled in the distance. If she had to die in this awful place, she hoped it would be quick.

Seconds passed. Nothing happened.

The Bygone spoke up, faintly amused. "Tell me, mortal. What do you think I plan to do to you?"

Ruby opened her eyes and stifled a shriek.

He was looming over her. Shadows crept out from under his mask, brushing her cheek. They weren't cold like she expected. But they weren't warm either. They felt like... nothing. Little strips of nothing curling over her cheek.

The Bygone's jaw dropped open. A devastatingly long, pink tongue dripped out of his mouth and trailed along her neck.

Ruby drew in a ragged breath. But before she could scream, his tongue slipped back into his mouth.

"Mortal," he rumbled. "I asked you a question."

Ruby flinched. "You're... you're going to eat me?"

The Bygone hummed again like he had been thinking about it. But before Ruby could brace herself, the shadows retreated behind his mask.

He turned away.

"Little witch," he commanded, not bothering to glance back as he stalked through the shadowy trees. "Follow me."

Two

The mortal stared at the portal that was fizzing in the middle of the shadowy tree like it was going to attack her.

"Where are we going?" she asked timidly.

"Nowhere," Slate replied. "We are waiting for someone to come to us."

"Oh." The mortal swallowed, fidgeting with her thick cloak. "Who?"

"My brother," Slate replied, his tail flicking in irritation. "Do you always ask so many annoying questions?"

She fell silent—for about five seconds.

"Did you steal him?"

"The dog spirit?" he realized. "No. Why do you look surprised?"

The witch attempted to wipe the shock off her face. "It's just... what you do. Right? The dreaded Bygone, stealing people from forest paths. Then you eat them."

Slate laughed, making the witch jump.

"Is that what they told you?" Slate asked. "I am a *guide*. This is the void of wanderers. I lead souls where they are supposed to be. When I must eat, I do it outside my void."

Unless you didn't bind me, he thought. *Then I would have had you for breakfast.*

The mortal was quiet again, to his relief.

Still, he couldn't help but admire her annoying spirit. Most mortals he interacted with screamed at the sight of him. And she was clearly scared, evident by her trembling frame. But she kept meeting his eye, and her hand was steady around her chipped dagger.

He let his gaze travel over her once more: long ebony hair, surprisingly inky eyes. A dark cloak and skin almost as pale as him. Framed against his forest, she almost looked like she belonged there.

Then he noticed the blood in her cheeks. Heard her heartbeat fluttering in her flushed chest and tasted her salty sweat in the crisp evening air. Her cloak wasn't black at all; it was a deep brown. She was pretty for a mortal. And she smelled good enough to eat.

If only she hadn't bound him. Now, he had to complete his half of the deal.

If she still wants to do it after she learns what is needed, he reminded himself.

He adjusted his loincloth. He hadn't straightened it in... several centuries, at least. Granted, he had been asleep for most of that time.

Something the mortal had said niggled at him.

"That name," he said. "What did you call me?"

"The... Bygone?" The mortal frowned. "Is that not your name?"

Slate had never heard that word in the entirety of his long existence. Before he could answer, the portal pulsed. A Skullstalker stepped out of the flaming door. He had huge horns and spiked wings tucked into his back.

"Brother," Wick greeted as the portal whirled in the dark tree behind him. "I thought you were sleeping through this century."

Slate growled. "Something incredibly irritating woke me up."

"Oh?" Wick's fiery eyes landed on the witch. "Who is this?"

Slate ignored him. It hardly mattered, mortals died too quickly to bother learning their names.

"Paimon has not been answering his followers," he said.

"Paimon? Huh." Wick frowned, gaze dragging back to the mortal. "Slate, who *is* this? She smells like..."

He leaned in, sniffing her long, dark hair. The witch stiffened, her hand twitching around her bloody dagger.

"Back," she said, her voice breaking. She cleared her throat. "Get back."

Wick blinked, stepping back. "Why is this mortal bound to you, Slate? Is she a sacrifice?"

"They have not sacrificed anyone to me in centuries," Slate said, annoyed. He quite missed the mortal sacrifices. He would untie them and let them try to escape first. He never got to chase the lost souls who ended up in his realm, so it was fun to finally give in to the hunt.

Slate pushed the fond memories away. "Have you heard from Paimon?"

Wick shook his head. "No. Out of all of us, I would have expected *you* to know."

Slate hummed. It was a fair enough expectation, once. But things had changed. Nothing dramatic, obviously—they just drifted apart. Paimon was getting annoying, always intruding on his void and waking him up. Slate had been relieved when he stopped. Now he was thinking maybe he should have been worried.

"Have fun with your not-sacrifice," Wick said.

"Go away, Wick."

Wick shrugged and stepped back through the portal.

"Good to meet you," Wick called as it closed behind him. "I hope he doesn't eat you!"

"Thanks," the mortal called back, sounding bewildered.

The portal sealed shut. The mortal gasped, reaching out like she was going to touch the bark it had closed on.

Slate considered. He knew all of Paimon's hidden places. He could seek them out and avoid the ritual altogether. He doubted she would want to do it in the first place. Mortals were so small, after all. It would be difficult, maybe impossible, for them to mate.

And importantly, he *did* want to know where Paimon had snuck off to.

He opened his mouth to tell her to stay put.

She cut him off. "What did he say about you sleeping through the century?"

"What of it?"

She frowned. "Why sleep through a century?"

"Why not? There is not much to do around here. If a soul shows up, I will sense it and guide it out." Slate's tail swished uncomfortably. He didn't encounter these questions often. He didn't encounter *any* questions lately—he was too busy sleeping.

He smoothed his loincloth. "Stay here. I must attend to something."

"Wait!" She moved like she was going to step in front of him, then faltered. "Why am I here? I-I thought—"

"You thought I would eat you," he finished.

She nodded faintly. She was still flushed with prey-animal fear, her skin shimmering with sweat. She had been convinced he would eat her. And she still came.

Slate was rarely impressed by mortals. He was surprised to find himself impressed now. Not fully—he felt very few emotions fully nowadays—but a hint of it.

He turned to her, watching her pulse thrum against her delicate throat. "I thought of it. But something stopped me."

She swallowed. "What?"

He stepped closer. "Do you know what renewing Paimon's protection ward entails?"

"No," she admitted.

"It requires an old and powerful magic. A mating ritual."

"*Oh.*" Her eyelids fluttered, and Slate thought, for some reason, of the spiderwebs in his forest, sloughing shadows from their threads.

"Mating," she whispered. "You mean... lying together?"

He nodded. He waited for the screaming to start or for her to say she would rather leave her town to die and start anew somewhere else. Mortals despised Skullstalkers, after all. Especially the ones they feared so much they gave special names—*the Bygone.* The last time he was in the mortal realm, they had no name for him at all.

The witch lifted her chin to meet his eyes again.

"If that's what it takes," she said softly. "When do we start?"

Slate hesitated. Something was stirring in his gut. He was surprised when he realized it was desire. He had spent so long slumbering the years away and half-heartedly ruling his void to feel much of anything, let alone desire for another creature. He had not expected it to happen because of the witch in front of him, all dark hair and flushed skin, chest heaving under her plain mortal dress.

"Soon," he promised. "I must search for Paimon. Perhaps he is lost or trapped."

"Did you..." She squinted up at him. "*Know* him?"

For an odd moment, Slate considered telling her the whole story. Then he was reminded how useless it was to tell anything to a mortal and stopped.

"I do," he said instead.

He turned for the door.

"Wait," she repeated. This time, she really did step in front of him, black leaves crunching under her boots.

"That other Skullstalker called you 'Slate.' Is that your name? Your real one?"

Slate hadn't realized humans had forgotten. It must have been a very long time since he visited the mortal realm.

"It is," he allowed.

She nodded. A strand of raven hair fell over her face, catching on her lip.

"I'm Ruby," she said in a rush. Like she was afraid to give it but determined all the same. Just like everything else she had done since stepping through that portal into his void.

"What will you have of me?" the witch continued. "After you grant me my boon."

He watched the stray lock of hair resting over her lip. Another urge rose in him, just as powerful as the urge to lunge and devour her whole: he wanted to reach out and brush the hair from her face.

"I haven't decided yet," he said.

THREE

Ruby woke up cold and alone on the forest floor.

It was still evening. At least, it *looked* like evening. But it couldn't be. She had walked through the forest for hours before finally giving in and curling up against a tree.

Maybe the forest went on forever. That was what she heard, anyway. But, apparently, childhood stories weren't as reliable as she thought.

She sat up, tightening her cloak around her shivering shoulders. A *guide*. She had never heard of the Bygone as a guide. Just an evil Skullstalker, luring victims to their doom.

Apparently, they had gotten much wrong about him. He hadn't even *heard* of a Bygone. What else had they made up about him over the generations?

Ruby touched her cheek. Slate's tongue had been massive, pink, and long as it trailed down her face. If *everything* about him was that big, she couldn't see how they could ever complete a mating ritual.

Maybe he'll force it in, whispered a worried voice at the back of her head. *Maybe he'll split you open.*

The words sent a strange heat pooling between her legs, the same thrill that had started when he loomed over her that first time. There was fear there, of course. But there was also something else... She had dreamed of it last night: the loincloth pooling on the forest floor. Those huge hands prying her thighs apart, claws pricking into her tender skin, those black eyes boring into hers as he pushed inside, impossibly big.

She supposed her nervous excitement didn't matter. The thrill would fade once the agonizing pain set in.

Ruby's stomach growled. She hadn't brought any rations with her. She had assumed she would be dead before she needed them.

She stood and cleared her throat timidly. "I don't suppose there are any lost souls around who can point me toward some food or water?"

Silence. Ruby sighed and started walking, glad that she had brought her sturdy boots.

She had barely made it two steps before something rustled in a nearby bush.

Ruby froze, her hand flying into her dress pocket to grab her dagger. "Hello?"

The dog spirit burst out of the bush, its tail wagging.

Ruby sagged with relief. "You almost gave me a heart attack! Where have you been?"

The dog spirit ambled up, tongue lolling. It gave

Ruby's knee a friendly nudge, and Ruby smiled in wonder at the strange, light weight of its furry head. If they were in the human realm, its head would have gone right through her knee.

She stroked the dog spirit, her smile growing at the barely-there sensation of its fur. "You don't happen to know where I can find some food, do you?"

The dog spirit sat back and cocked its head.

"Didn't think so," Ruby said. "Want to come, anyway?"

The dog spirit barked, tail wagging harder.

Ruby laughed and led it further into the forest.

She sat down sometime later with a meal of bright orange eggs, surprised to find her fear had died down to a low simmer.

The dog spirit helped. Its cheerful disposition made the shadowy trees look less terrifying.

The flames she had used to heat the rocks started to die. Ruby pointed at it, and the flames soared so high she startled and had to lean back.

She was even more powerful in the Bygone's void than in the mortal realm. It didn't make sense. Then again, apparently, she didn't know as much as she thought. The Bygone didn't lure souls to their doom; he guided them out of it. Neither Skullstalker she'd met had eaten her. Mating rituals weren't a rumor. And nothing in this terrifying forest had attacked her yet.

The dog spirit barked, resting its head on her knee and wagging its tail hopefully.

"You don't even need to eat," she told it. She poked at the orange eggs, which had crisped up nicely on the heated rocks. "What do you think, will these turn me into a frog?"

The dog spirit licked its chops.

Ruby sighed. Then she tucked a piece of egg into her mouth.

It tasted... fine. A little spicy, which she wasn't used to. But otherwise, it tasted like any normal egg. And the more she chewed, the more she enjoyed the spice.

She was halfway through the second egg when a voice spoke up behind her.

"Mortal. What are you doing?"

Ruby shrieked and whirled around.

Slate loomed above her, his frown visible below his skull mask.

The dog spirit barked and jumped up at him enthusiastically.

Ruby eyed him worriedly, waiting for Slate to smite it. Or banish it. Or whatever Slate did to spirits that annoyed him. For all he called himself a 'guide,' he had confessed to wanting to eat her earlier.

But Slate only pushed the dog off with a distracted frown. Then, to her surprise, he gave the dog a pat behind its ears. He even retracted his claws, the dog whining happily under his touch.

Ruby wiped spicy grease off her mouth. "I... I found these eggs. Is that okay?"

Slate didn't respond. He was staring at her with an expression she couldn't identify. He was still petting the dog, looming over her so closely she could see the grooves in his white horns.

Then she noticed his lips part. His fangs glinted beneath them, impossibly sharp.

He's hungry, Ruby realized with a jolt of cold fear. *He's thinking of eating me again.*

She stepped back warily. "Slate?"

Slate blinked, startled. Then he straightened. "Why were you hungry? It hasn't been long since I left."

Ruby sagged with relief. Nobody was getting eaten today.

"With all due respect," she said carefully. "It's been at least a night."

"Has it? Hmm." Slate looked toward the blue flames. They went out immediately, and Ruby tried not to be disappointed. She had enjoyed playing with her suddenly powerful magic.

He held out a hand. "Come."

Ruby eyed his long fingers cautiously. "Where are we going this time?"

"To my castle."

"Castle," Ruby blurted. She looked around the forest she just spent the night in, cold and uncomfortable. He had a *castle*?

"Yes," Slate said impatiently. "I must prepare you for the ritual."

Ruby shivered. Last night's dream drifted back, imagining those sharp fangs trailing over her skin.

"Little witch," Slate said impatiently.

Ruby shook herself out of the shameful daydream. "Yes! Sorry, yes."

She slipped her hand into his. His fingers were huge and cool, his claws pressing gently into her skin. His hand utterly enveloped hers, and not for the first time, Ruby was consumed by the idea of him holding her down. He would cover her completely. She would be helpless.

It terrified her. It excited her. But, before she could decide what she thought about it, he turned away from her and led her out of the forest.

It took a surprisingly short amount of time for the castle to reveal itself.

Ruby gasped and came to a stumbling stop.

The castle was huge, with giant black spires stretching toward an ever-darkening sky.

It wasn't *decaying*. Not quite. But it was coming close. Moss crept over the walls, and vines worked stubbornly through the stones, spilling shadows. It was obvious the Bygone—*Slate*, she reminded herself—didn't take much care of this place.

"Mortal," Slate prompted, irritated. He tugged at her hand, as he had done several times throughout the walk whenever she dared walk too slow.

Ruby resumed her brisk pace and determinedly didn't shudder as she passed the crumbling doorway.

Slate led her through a maze of twisting hallways.

They turned so many corners Ruby stopped trying to keep track of where they were going.

Finally, he pulled her into a dark, cavernous room lined wall to floor with dirt-streaked stones.

Only then did he let go of her hand. It flexed at his side, his tail lashing. Ruby expected him to berate her for walking so slowly, but he said nothing for so long that it made her wonder if he was talking himself out of eating her again.

"Strip," he said finally. "I will fetch the ritual oil."

Ruby fought a blush. Of course, she would need to be naked, what else had she expected?

"Of course," she mumbled. She wanted to keep meeting his eyes, prove she wasn't afraid of him, but her gaze fell to the sleek floor as she untied her cloak.

Slate turned and walked out a door into a hallway that looked just as broken as this room.

The door was massive, Ruby noted. Like the rest of the castle, it was much bigger than a Skullwalker required. Maybe Skullwalkers like their architecture to be twice their already huge size.

Ruby unlaced her dress and thought back to the nest she'd found him in front of. The feather he had woven through it, the fur lining the edges. *That* he took care of. In contrast, the castle was falling apart.

Ruby pulled off her dress and shivered. This room was even colder than the forest. She clutched her clothes to her chest, trying to find someplace to set them down that wasn't covered in filth or plant matter.

The giant door opened. Ruby jumped, dropping her bundle to the mossy stones.

If Slate noticed her nakedness, he didn't show it. He placed a bowl of viscous blue liquid on a nearby table, which—much like the door—also looked too tall for him.

Slate dipped his fingers into the dark liquid and drew them out dripping. Then he turned to her and stopped.

"Arms down," he instructed.

Ruby looked down. She had been covering her breasts. She hadn't noticed.

She lowered her arms, fighting back a shiver. She was breaking out in goosebumps. Hopefully, he thought it was the icy air and not her racing heartbeat or the giddy lurch in her stomach that was only partly fear.

She took a deep breath and raised her eyes.

Slate was staring down at her, as she knew he would be. His face was unreadable behind his skull mask, but his *eyes...*

Her breath caught. People in her town glanced at her, at best. They never looked at her like the world was narrowing down into her. He still looked hungry, but there was something else in his expression now. She couldn't tell what.

"Good," Slate said quietly. Then he paused like he hadn't meant to say that. He lifted his dripping fingers to her face and retracted his claws. "Hold still."

She swallowed, her dry throat clicking. "Wait!"

His fingers paused an inch away from her cheek. "Yes?"

"Can..." She swallowed again. "Can I have some water? I'm thirsty."

The shadows leaking out from his mask flickered. His tail swished, and Ruby thought of the unfriendly stray cats who lined up at her door asking for food but denying her pats.

"*Mortals,*" he muttered dismissively.

But he set the bowl back on the table and left the room, reappearing a surprisingly short time later with a chalice of water. The chalice—like the table and the door—was *also* far too big for him. It made Ruby wonder if this castle was ever meant for Skullwalkers at all. That being said, she didn't know any creature bigger than a Skullstalker who had the capabilities to *want* a castle, let alone be able to make one.

Ruby reached for it, only to stop when he held it up to her lips.

"Open," he said.

Ruby let her mouth fall open. He tipped the water into her mouth, and Ruby gulped as best she could. But it was too much. Water rolled down her chin and her neck.

"Sorry," she said, her mind flurrying. Why was *she* apologizing?

Slate grunted as he watched a drop slide over her hardening nipple. It sounded like branches breaking.

"Interesting," he grumbled.

"What?"

"Your body." Slate placed the mug down and dipped two fingers into the dark blue liquid again. "One touch and it changes. Your skin slicks with sweat, and your pupils swell. I haven't seen it since I last ate one of you."

Ruby's heart thudded painfully in her chest as she imagined him pinning her down in that dark forest. Those sharp claws shredding her dress from chest to thigh, that big, long tongue down her belly—

Slate pressed his wet fingers against her cheek.

Ruby gasped. His fingers were cool and slick, moving in short lines as he decorated her face. It was, she realized with a hot sense of humiliation, the most intimate anyone had been with her since the last witch of Sweetsguard died. She almost wished he would be rough with her. He was touching her so gently that she wanted to thank him for it.

She blinked back the heat behind her eyes. "Is there... is there any news about Paimon?"

"Nothing." He stroked a line down her nose. "It is like he vanished."

He sounded frustrated. She frowned.

"Were you...?" Ruby jolted as he traced a line over her breast. His touch filled her with hot anticipation and deep worry. "Um, were you close?"

She expected him to brush her off. His tail swished again, irritated.

"Once," he admitted grudgingly.

Ruby thought that was the end of that. She closed her eyes, forcing herself not to shiver as his fingers ran a circle around her belly button.

Then Slate asked, "How long have you worshipped him?"

Ruby's eyes flew open. Was he really trying to make conversation right now?

"My whole life," Ruby replied. "He takes care of my town. That's all I want to do."

Slate rumbled low in his throat. It sounded very close to a laugh. But—shockingly—not a dismissive one. He cut it off quickly, his gaze darting back to where he was tracing swirling patterns over her trembling belly.

"You must care for your town very much."

Ruby smiled tightly. "I do."

Even if they don't care for me, she finished silently.

Slate's wet fingers dragged dark blue lines down her stomach, down and down, until they touched the thick hair between her legs.

Ruby held her breath, her eyes slamming shut once more. She was embarrassingly wet; she could feel it on her thighs. Even with all that slick, she had no idea how he would fit inside her. A finger, she could take. Probably. His fingers were so much thicker than hers. But any more? She had no clue.

Slate's fingers vanished.

Ruby opened her eyes just in time to see Slate brush his wet thumb over her lower lip.

"It is finished," he said. His thumb lingered, the barest hint of a claw sliding out to press into the sensitive skin. Slate swayed forward, and Ruby heard herself gasp. Was he going to kiss her or take a bite out of her cheek?

Then Slate straightened, his tail lashing furiously behind him.

"Finished," he repeated, looking away. "Come along."

He held out a hand. His claws were fully out again, and Ruby pictured them pressing into her naked hips.

He led her into a forest clearing. It was still evening, the shadowy trees glinting in the low light.

A familiar slab of stone sat in the middle of the long grass.

"The ward," Ruby realized. She dropped his hand and stepped closer, fighting the urge to close her arms over her naked body. It looked the same as it did in the middle of town: the stone was strained and brittle, and the ram horn symbol faded to the point of unrecognition.

She ran her fingers over the ruined symbol. It pulsed under her touch, and she gasped as it flowed through her.

This was going to work. It *had* to work. She had never felt so powerful, so *connected*—

Slate's shadow fell over her. "Are you ready, little witch?"

"Yes," Ruby whispered. "What should I do?"

She turned and stammered to a stop.

His loincloth was gone. The Bygone stood before her, bare and glorious. His horns jutted proudly from the top of his skull mask, his fangs visible between his parted lips. His tail swept back and forth in the dead leaves.

She suddenly wished she could see the rest of his face. She could tell nothing from the lower half after the skull mask ended: his mouth was straight and impassive, betraying nothing but boredom.

As if on a fishhook, Ruby's gaze fell to his cock.

It was *huge*. So huge that Ruby shuddered in equal parts excitement and terror. But even *that* wasn't the worrying part.

She pointed at the thick ridge circling the base of his cock. "What is *that*?"

"My knot," he replied. "You will have to take it to complete the ritual."

Ruby's heart thumped. Knot or otherwise, she couldn't squeeze that inside her.

She suddenly wished she *had* given in to those stupid boys cajoling her into "a good time" back home. Maybe if she had more experience, she could take more than her own fingers, and she wouldn't be staring at his cock with something that bordered on despair.

Slate tilted his head. "You look shocked. Do mortals not have knots?"

"They don't," Ruby squeaked. "But that's... that's fine. Everything's good."

He grunted and motioned toward the ward. "Bend over the stone."

The words sent a thrill through her, even as nervous sweat dripped down her neck. She suddenly wished he had grabbed her and thrown her down onto it.

She turned back and bent over the flat stone. It pressed against her breasts, smearing the blue liquid he had traced over her body.

Slate stepped up behind her. His huge hand stroked down her spine, gathering sweat.

Interesting, Ruby remembered him saying.

She gasped as that hand stroked down between her legs, pulling them gently apart.

Something prodded at her entrance, and she tensed. But it wasn't the impossible stretch of his cock pressing into her. It was his finger, claws thankfully retracted.

"I do not know much about humans," Slate admitted, sounding oddly hesitant. He pressed his finger shallowly inside. "You will... stretch. Correct?"

Ruby laughed hoarsely. She was shaking, she couldn't stop it. His finger felt strange but so *good* inside her, pumping lazily as he waited for her response.

"We do," she whispered. "We do stretch."

"Good. You will need to."

His finger disappeared. Something else brushed against her opening instead, so huge that Ruby gasped.

Her clit throbbed. Even as she waited for the pain to start, she couldn't deny the effect this was having on her. If only he would touch her again. A hand on her back, an arm wrapped underneath her breasts. Fangs on her neck, tail wrapping around her leg, his strange voice panting in her ear—

But the only touch she got was a clawed hand on her hip, wrapping around almost her entire torso as he pushed inside.

Or tried to.

Ruby couldn't hide her wince at the blunt intrusion

at her entrance. It wasn't going in, but the pressure stung.

Slate growled. "When does the stretching begin?"

Ruby's eyes prickled with pained tears. "Any s-second now."

Slate pushed more insistently. The narrowest point of his cock slipped inside.

Ruby bit her lip to muffle a cry. The heat between her legs was gone, replaced by a shooting pain she had never known.

Her fingers dug into the crumbling stone. She had to take his knot to complete the ritual. But how could she if she couldn't even take the head?

Suddenly, the painful pressure was gone.

"Why are you weeping?" Slate asked, annoyed. "Are mortals supposed to weep when they mate?"

"No, it's—" Ruby sniffed, trying to stop the tears from slipping down her cheeks. "I'm fine. You can keep going."

She dropped her forehead to the stone ward, waiting. But the pressure didn't come back.

Slate dropped her hip. The soft sting of his claws disappearing felt like failure.

"Wait!" Ruby turned, wiping her wet cheeks. "I can do it! I promise!"

"You cannot," he said. "Why did you tell me it was possible? And why are you still weeping?"

"What? I'm not! I'm just—" Ruby wiped her face more desperately. "I feel stupid."

"Why?" Slate frowned. "It is not your fault you are

small and weak. It *is* your fault you lied to me. Why bother asking for a ritual you cannot complete?"

Ruby hugged her arms, trying not to feel like such a failure. But it was difficult when she was standing naked in front of a monster who hadn't even been able to fit his cockhead inside her.

"It's not just because I'm small. It's also..." She sighed, bracing herself. "I've never done this before."

Four

Slate opened his mouth to exasperatedly point out that, of *course*, she had never performed a mating ritual with a Skullstalker. He'd never heard of it happening before in all his long existence.

Then it struck him.

He frowned. "You have never had anything inside you before?"

Ruby sniffled and nodded. Her face was blotchy and wet, disappointed tears clinging to her spiderweb eyelashes. He fought down the urge to lick them off her cheeks. If he gave in, he would be all the more tempted to take a proper bite, and the binding forbade it.

He considered her small stature. She had been partly truthful about stretching; he had managed to force a small part of himself inside. But it was nowhere near enough to fit all of him, let alone his knot.

Which she had obviously known. She hadn't

sounded surprised when he was unable to fit, only desperate. It made sense if she had never had anything inside her before.

He stepped back, tail swishing in annoyance. "This isn't going to work."

Ruby's tearful eyes went wide. She took a determined step toward him. "No! It has to! My town—"

He cut her off with an irritated growl. "I am not saying it can *never* work. I am saying we need to prepare."

She frowned, looking down at the smeared lines over her naked body. "You mean… more oil?"

"No." Slate dropped to his knees in front of her. She was so small he barely had to look up to meet her eyes, even from his knees. "I mean, you need something inside you. Something smaller than my cock. Have you even bothered to use your tiny mortal fingers?"

Ruby's cheeks flushed harder, and Slate's gaze dragged down to the redness blotching over her chest.

His mouth watered. Slate swallowed the gush of saliva, surprised. He rarely had involuntary physical reactions these days. He thought the shiver that had run through his tail when she took his hand earlier had been a fluke. But now it was happening again.

"I have," Ruby whispered.

It took Slate a moment to remember what she was replying to.

"Good," he said gruffly. "That is better than nothing, I guess."

Ruby dug her pointless mortal teeth into her lip. "What are you going to do to me?"

Slate considered. Then he picked her up and set her down on the stone slab, ignoring her startled yelp.

He pulled her legs open, another gush of saliva filling his mouth as he saw her puffy entrance. She smelled wet; he had caught this scent back in the room where he'd anointed her. Sweet and inviting, like it was calling him to bury his tongue inside.

Do not eat her, he reminded himself. *No matter how much you wish to.*

He pressed his nose to her thigh and inhaled, breathing in her musky scent. He didn't even care that she was pulling these uninvited reactions from him anymore. Not when they felt so good. He had been sleeping for so long he had forgotten the delights wakefulness could offer.

Ruby squeaked. He looked up to see her staring at him, her chest heaving.

"What is it?" he asked. "Do you have some better idea to make me fit, tiny human?"

"No," she said, very fast.

He turned back to her entrance. A pearl of liquid clung to her lips. He let his tongue unfurl, the long length sliding against her folds.

"Oh, *gods!*" Ruby's legs closed around his head. "That's so... *ohhhh.*"

There was a small nub peeking out at the top of her folds. He swiped his tongue over it curiously, gratified when Ruby yelled and stretched out over the stone, her spine a satisfying arch.

Slate trailed his tongue down and pressed inside.

Unlike his cock, it went in with little fuss. She was still incredibly tight, but there was no pain in her voice as he thrust his tongue deeper.

She tasted divine. It was suddenly difficult to remind himself that he was not allowed to eat her. Every instinct inside him told him to hold her down and dig his teeth in. Then Ruby cried out with pleasure, and the urge to devour her was replaced by the urge to coax more noises out of her flushed throat.

Slate thrust his tongue deeper, basking in the sweet taste. He couldn't remember why he hadn't participated in the pleasures of the flesh for so long. He hadn't partaken in anything except for slumber for a long, long time. He hadn't even noticed Paimon's ward growing old and weak. A thousand years ago, he would have noticed the very first chip in the stone. Then again, a thousand years ago, Paimon would have been around to notice it for him, the annoying little goat god.

Ruby's walls fluttered around him. There was a part inside her that was a different texture than the rest, and he rubbed the point of his tongue over it.

Ruby cried out, grabbing onto his horns. "*Gods!*"

More sweet liquid rushed to meet his tongue. Slate lapped it up, dimly aware that his cock had not gone down like he had told it to when he realized she was too small to fit him. Instead, it was throbbing, even *leaking*. Slate hummed in annoyance as he felt pearly liquid drip down his shaft and onto his swelling knot.

Ruby's legs went rigid around him at the vibrations.

Her hips bucked, her clit grazing the edge of his skull mask.

Ruby yelled. Another gush of liquid soaked Slate's tongue, more copious than the last. Slate lapped at it, sucking it out of her hole with a narrow-minded determination he had not felt for an age. It filled his head like a spell, huge and intoxicating. For a moment, nothing mattered in any realm except making her tremble around his tongue.

Finally, Ruby sagged against the warding stone, a triumphant smile quivering on her face.

"Are you sure that didn't work?" she panted. "It felt... effective."

"I am sure," he replied. "You must take my knot to renew the ward."

He slipped a finger inside her. Ruby jerked, her heel bumping into his shoulder blades.

The first finger fit well. The *second* finger was a strain, and he could hear Ruby holding back a pained hiss.

So small, Slate thought. He wanted to be annoyed at her for offering herself up for a ritual she knew she couldn't complete. But for some reason, he couldn't muster the irritation. He watched her tight hole stretch around his fingers, her legs shaking with effort.

"I think..." Ruby swallowed. "How long will we do this? I don't know if..."

She trailed off. He heard it anyway: mortals could not keep doing one thing for long. They needed *rest* and *food* and *water* all the time, like some baby Skullstalker whose skull mask was still soft and rubbery.

He sighed and stood, noticing with some surprise that his cock was *still* hard and leaking. He picked up his loincloth and knotted it over his erection.

"Come," he said impatiently. "We can prepare more after you have rested. I assume you need rest?"

"Yes," she said, sounding surprised. Her gaze darted down toward the bulge in his robes.

He willed his cock to go soft. It was a simple enough request. But it stayed stubbornly erect. It even spasmed, a tiny wet patch forming at the tip.

Ruby made a soft noise in her throat. "Are you sure you don't want... anything else?"

Slate wanted little. He wanted to eat her. He wanted to be left alone. He wanted to rest. He wanted to take care of his void, though that got less important over the millennia. If a lost soul appeared, he sensed it, woke up, took care of it, and returned to his slumber. Easy.

Slate considered what she was offering. It would be pleasurable, letting her service him. And yet, there was something uncomfortable about being so driven by these desires. He had so few. Not to mention these desires transcended the physical; beyond his throbbing cock was a deep craving he could not name, a need deeper than hunger. He suspected that if he gave in to her, that nameless craving would only grow.

"No," he told her.

"Oh." Her legs came together, her brow wrinkling. "Alright."

She rubbed her arms. Cold again, he realized, just like she had been when he anointed her. Were humans *always* cold? He could not fathom an existence of constant eating, drinking, sleeping, and warming oneself. How did they have time for anything else in their short existence?

"Come," he said again, rolling his eyes. "I will take you somewhere warm."

He took them to a bedroom. There were many in the castle, all of them covered in dust from centuries of disuse.

She ran her hand along a dusty coverlet and coughed, waving the puff of dust out of her face. "If you have this castle, why sleep in the forest?"

"It is more comfortable in the forest," he replied, giving the bed a dismissive look. "No reasonable Skull-stalker would bother sleeping on *that*."

"Right," Ruby said distractedly. She stroked the coverlet again. For a moment, he thought she was brushing off the dust. Then he noticed the wonder in her eyes and remembered how small these mortal lives were. She had probably never been outside of her little town before, let alone her realm.

It made him feel... *something*, watching her stoke the soft material. He didn't quite know what, but it was flickering warmly in his chest.

Ruby shivered again.

"It is not *that* cold," Slate argued. "Here, I will light a fire."

He turned to the fireplace. But before he could summon any flames, the fireplace roared to life in a flash of familiar blue, so powerful Slate had to jump back to avoid being singed.

Slate turned. Ruby was staring, eyes wide and hands extended, at the flames she had just conjured.

Slate snorted. "Powerful little witch."

"I'm sorry," she blurted. "Did I get you?"

"You would have to work harder to harm me." Slate brushed down his loincloth, subtly checking it for any signs of charring.

"My magic was getting weaker with Paimon gone. But... it's so strong here." Ruby gazed into the blue flames with a strange expression. Worry, to be sure. But also eagerness.

Maybe she does want power, after all, Slate thought. But her eagerness didn't look like she was thinking about what havoc she could wreak with her newfound strength. It was... oddly wondrous.

No mortal had ever looked at this void with wonder. No mortal had *been* to his void unless they were dead or horrendously lost and in need of a quick exit.

Ruby straightened, her arms coming up to cover her bare chest. "Thank you for bringing me here. Do you, by any chance, have a bath?"

"I have a pond," Slate said dryly.

"Oh. That will do."

Slate sighed. The mortal looked so sad, standing there all naked and shivering.

"I also have a bath," he admitted grudgingly.

• • •

He led her to a bathroom that was even more dusty than the bedroom.

Slate examined the silver faucets cautiously. It had been a long time since he had used them. He preferred to bathe in the pond unless there was ice on the ground. Then, he dragged himself into this wretched castle and took advantage of the magic that had been cast on it long before he was born.

He twisted a faucet. Water clattered into the claw-foot tub.

Ruby gasped as steam rose into the air. "It flows *hot?*"

"It does."

"That's incredible." Ruby reached over the large tub, a shocked laugh spilling out of her mouth as she touched the gushing faucet.

Slate watched her, oddly charmed. Her laugh was so bright he almost expected the shadows clinging to his skull mask to shy away. Then he caught a flash of black out of the corner of his eye and noticed something even more shocking: they were stretching out toward her. A tendril brushed her bare ankle, curling around the knob of bone.

Ruby yelped, jumping high. High for a mortal, anyway.

Get back. Slate tugged his shadows close, annoyed and confused. Since when did his shadows start reaching out to random mortals? Even on the rare occasion that he got to eat one, his shadows barely flickered in their direction.

"I will leave you to your rest," he said, turning hastily for the door.

"Slate?"

He turned back. Ruby was sitting on the edge of the bath, curled over her bare body as if he had not seen it splayed out over the warding stone. As if he had not held her thighs open while he buried his tongue inside that tight, wet heat.

"Thank you," Ruby said softly. "You are... not what I expected."

Slate was annoyed, imagining the tales she must have heard from humans who had not heard his real name in generations. Everything the mortal realm heard from the voids was secondhand information at best, passed down through so many mouths it was close to worthless.

Then again... she was right to be scared. He was a Skullstalker, after all. He guided lost souls in his void, but if he encountered one in another void, they were as good as breakfast.

When he bothered to eat, anyhow. He hadn't needed to in decades. He had not felt a pang of genuine hunger until Ruby stumbled into his void, flushed and slick with sweat.

"Neither are you, little witch," he told her.

He turned to leave once more.

"Slate," Ruby repeated, sounding much stiffer.

He turned back to find her looking embarrassed.

"Do you think you could find my clothes?" she asked quietly.

Slate considered her naked appearance and wanted to

argue. She looked good like this, all smooth and soft, not hidden by all that thick fabric. But she also looked deeply uncomfortable. If she was going to be stuck in his void for a while, she would have to wear something.

Just not those clothes.

"I will find you something better," he promised.

FIVE

S late was still gone when Ruby climbed out of the bathtub.

Ruby wound a thick, fluffy towel around her body and waited. But she was getting cold again, and the demon was nowhere to be seen.

She bit her lip, considering. Nothing in this realm had hurt her yet. And Slate hadn't told her to stay put. What harm could come from trying to find him?

She stepped into the cool hallway and stifled a shriek.

The dog spirit was waiting for her, tail wagging furiously.

"You scared the skin off of me," Ruby gasped. She adjusted her towel and bent down to pet the dog, her hand almost pressing through its translucent fur. "Are you allowed in here, boy? I don't want you to get in trouble."

The dog spirit licked her hand, unbothered.

Ruby kept stroking, lost in thought. "Is he kind to you? He seems..."

She trailed off uncertainly. It wasn't like she *trusted* him. But for all his monstrous traits—horns and fangs and tail and huge black eyes, his dripping tongue, and his hungry gaze like he was constantly holding himself back from eating her—he hadn't done anything monstrous. He had her completely at his mercy. He could do *anything* to her. And he had decided to...

...run her a bath and find her some new clothes.

Ruby had meant for him to find the clothes she'd left in the anointment room, but he had said he would find something more suitable. Whatever *that* meant.

She looked down the hallway. It was long and narrow, the stone cold and plain under her feet. It had a surprising lack of decoration, not like the bedroom she had been shown earlier.

Ruby turned back to the dog spirit. "You don't happen to know where that bedroom is, do you?"

The dog spirit barked. Its ghostly teeth closed around her sleeve, tugging her down the hall.

"Oh," said Ruby. "Alright."

The dog spirit led her through crumbling hallway after crumbling hallway. Ruby tried to keep track this time, but she was never good at puzzles.

"If you're leading me to your food bowl," she began jokingly, stepping around a persistent drip that had carved a hole into the floor over the centuries.

The dog spirit made a muffled noise around her sleeve and stopped in front of a huge, dusty, ornate door.

Ruby eyed it. "You're sure?"

The dog spirit barked happily.

Ruby pushed the door. It took all her strength before it started to creak open, and Ruby sighed in relief at the bedroom he'd shown her earlier: the same giant, dusty bed, the same decrepit walls. The fireplace was still crackling as if no time had passed.

"For a spirit who's so good at finding things," she said as she crouched in front of the fire, fanning out her long dark hair to dry. "You'd think you'd be able to find your way to where you're meant to be."

The dog spirit sat down next to her. Spirits didn't feel the temperature in the mortal realm, but Ruby didn't know if that was the case here. The dog seemed content enough to lie down in front of the fire with its paws stretched out to catch the warm air.

She scratched behind its ears. "You're not meant to be here, you know. Someone's probably missing you."

The dog looked up at her, happy and uncomprehending.

"They are," she said. "They're waiting out there, somewhere. This realm isn't somewhere you stay. It's a place you wander before you figure out where you're meant to be. At least, that's what the Bygone... that's what *Slate* says."

She stared around the bedroom. Before Slate, she had never seen ceilings this tall. Never felt a water pump running hot. She had never seen trees dripping shadows or felt an inhumanly long tongue moving inside her.

It would all be over soon. Once he... *prepared* her properly, a thought that made Ruby's cheeks flush and her stomach fill with heat. Then, they would be able to complete the ritual, and Ruby would return to Sweetsguard. Go back to her cluttered cottage on the corner of town where nobody visited unless they wanted a boil lanced or a pregnancy gone or a love potion she politely refused to make.

The dog spirit nipped her hand good-naturedly and jumped up, sprinting to the other side of the room.

"If you want me to follow, I'm quite comfy here," she called.

The dog spirit whined and pawed at an obscenely tall wooden dresser.

"Is that where the Bygone keeps his treats?" Ruby grinned.

The dog spirit whined louder. Its paws kept scraping, and Ruby realized it was pawing pointedly at one specific drawer.

"*Is* that where he keeps his treats?" Ruby wondered and stood. She kept her towel secure around her chest as she crossed the room and bent down in front of the dresser, the dog spirit's whining turning excited as she reached for it.

"If you're luring me into a trap, I'll be very upset," Ruby warned him.

She opened the drawer. It took two hands to close around the handle.

It was empty except for a piece of paper folded in the corner, yellowing with age.

Ruby unfolded it. Two familiar faces stared up at her, sketched in charcoal: one of them was Slate, wearing a helmet on top of his skull mask and smiling so wide she could see all his fangs. And the other…

Ruby's breath hitched.

She knew that face. She had never *seen* it—not in its entirety—but she knew it deep in her bones.

"Paimon," she murmured.

The goat deity had a furry arm flung around Slate's shoulder, smiling just as hard. He was holding something in front of them. The paper was so faded it took Ruby a moment to realize what it was.

A demon head. Paimon was showing off a decapitated demon head.

Ruby winced. A sketch from after some gory battle. She had no idea which one; news rarely trickled from the voids into the mortal realms unless it affected humans. Any news that did come through was muddled with fiction and age. It could have been a battle that happened before her great-great-great-grandparents were born.

She turned the paper over. There was a line written in neat, swooping cursive: *cleaning up the wandering void with the goat.*

Ruby frowned. *Cleaning up?* Were there a lot of demons in Slate's realm? She'd never heard of that. She thought this realm was only for lost souls and unlucky travelers who wandered somewhere the veil was thin.

The dog spirit's ears pricked. It turned to the door, barking excitedly.

Ruby shoved the sketch back into the drawer and slammed it shut, her heart hammering.

The door opened. Slate stepped inside, looking utterly unsurprised to find her so far from the bathroom he'd left her in. He was holding a flowing black dress.

"This is for you," he announced. He laid the dress on the dusty coverlet.

Ruby stood, clutching her towel and trying to calm her thundering heartbeat. She could feel his unrelenting gaze upon her as she walked toward it.

Ruby reached cautiously for her towel. Slate had seen her lying naked over a stone slab. There was no reason for her to be self-conscious. But she couldn't help the hot shiver that ran through her as she let the towel drop to the floor.

She gathered the dress and let it fall over her head. The sleek fabric against her bare skin made her gasp. She was used to cotton and wool; she had never felt anything so luxurious. Not to mention the dark blue jewels studded down the leg, framing a slit down the side.

"I have a mirror," Slate offered.

He stepped back to reveal a mirror on the back of the bedroom door, towering over her.

She walked up to it and gaped.

Ruby stared at their reflection, a shaky realization coming over her. Her dress was the same shade as his robe. It could have been made from the same material, except no shadows were sloughing off her dress.

I look like I belong to him, she realized with a hot thrill.

Ruby ran a finger down the plunging neckline and shivered. Standing here below him, she looked like a devoted servant. Maybe a priestess. If her eyes got any darker, she could pass as his pet demon.

Or something even darker than that: she looked like something parents warned their children about. Like she should be dripping shadows right along with him.

Slate came up behind her. "Is it suitable?"

"Suitable," Ruby echoed faintly. "I... yes. Where did you even find this?"

"I crafted it myself," Slate replied. "I spun it out of shadows."

Ruby couldn't stop staring. Her stomach swooped. It felt like something huge had happened, only she didn't know what.

"Why this?" she whispered. "What was wrong with my dress?"

Slate huffed and looked away. The shadows around his mask flickered in irritation.

Ruby tensed, waiting to be told to stop talking. Gods knew she was used to it from her town.

"You are bound to a Skullstalker," Slate said finally, not meeting her eyes. "You should look like it."

Ruby swallowed. She still couldn't bring herself to tear her eyes away from her reflection.

"And *you* are bound to *me*," she said slowly, hardly believing her nerve even as she said it. "What should you look like?"

Her heart pounded, waiting for his response.

But Slate didn't growl. His tail didn't even sway in irritation. All of him stilled, even his shadows. Then he laughed, a clicking chirp that made her jump before she realized what it was.

"I am not in the mood to look small and weak," he said.

I don't look so small and weak now, Ruby thought, dazed.

"You said I was powerful," she said quietly. "When I lit the fire."

"Your *magic* is powerful. As it should be, away from that pale mortal realm." He hesitated, his claw grazing her sleeve. For a moment, it looked like he would say something else. Then he turned from her, his loincloth flowing over her dress.

"You must be getting hungry," he said dubiously.

Ruby laughed. He sounded so puzzled when he talked about human needs.

"Not yet," she said. "But soon, yes. I can find more eggs if you guide me back to the forest."

Slate snorted, rolling his shoulder in a way that reminded Ruby of wild animals crouching for a hunt.

"Don't bother. I will find you food." Slate turned toward the door, and Ruby's heart jerked in her chest as his reflection vanished from the mirror. For a moment, she'd almost felt... like she *was* something, which was ridiculous. She was the witch of Sweetsguard, protecting them from the edge of town. She was one of Paimon's worshippers, drawing her magic from his patronage.

This was something different. For a moment, she felt like she had tapped into something bigger, deeper, *darker*. A half-baked fantasy she didn't even know she had until he draped her in shadows and stood beside her.

She swallowed nervously. "Are... *you* getting hungry?"

Slate stopped at the bedroom doorway, the dog spirit on his heels. "If you are asking whether I will eat you, I cannot. And the hunger is..." He paused, frowning. "It is not a true hunger. I do not feel genuine hunger often. It is an opportunistic hunger, only conjured when I come across a mortal in the flesh."

"In the flesh," Ruby repeated. "As opposed to..."

"The mortals whom I encounter in this realm are usually dead," he replied. He cocked his head. "What do mortals eat?"

"Oh," Ruby said, suddenly forgetting everything she had ever eaten. It took her a moment to come up with: "Well, we eat meat. Eggs. Grains. Dairy. Dried fruit. *Fresh* fruit, when it's in season."

She paused, wondering whether to push her luck. But he'd made her a dress. Why not this?

"Chocolate," she said cautiously. "If you have it."

"I will find these items." His head inclined as if he was going to bow. Then it jerked back up in a strange almost-nod, and he headed into the hall.

The door thudded shut behind him. The dog spirit darted out after him, jumping through the closed door with a playful bark.

Ruby threw herself onto the bed, mind reeling. There was a part of her that kept expecting something horrible to happen: for those shadows trailing off his cloak to swarm up and swallow her, for his jaw to unhinge and expose a great red maw. *An opportunistic hunger,* he had admitted, *only conjured when I come across a mortal in the flesh.*

It wouldn't even be to fill his stomach. He would eat her out of pure want.

Ruby shivered. Even if he fed her and made her a dress, he was still dangerous. His fangs and his obvious interest in eating her proved that—not to mention the sketch of that bloody demon head proved that. She wished she still had her dagger, which was waiting for her with her old dress. Maybe she could find her way back to the anointing room somehow. The castle couldn't be *that* big.

Not that a dagger would do me much good, she thought as she remembered his massive stature and his huge fangs. But it would be better than nothing.

Even if she was starting to convince herself that she didn't have to worry about him.

She pushed the thought aside and blew out a shaky breath, shifting against the bed. The dress felt glorious against her bare skin.

She raised her leg through the slit. The dress puddled around it, revealing her leg up to her plump thigh. She touched the spot where the fabric parted and imagined Slate watching her, those dark eyes filled with a focus nobody had given her before.

She... *enjoyed* how he looked at her—even if it was mostly hunger. She liked it the same way she liked the dress: with a strange, murky excitement she didn't fully understand, even as it made heat pool in her stomach.

She slid a hand up the slit in her skirt until she was touching her core. It was swollen and sore at the entrance. Her clit was so sensitive she let out a hiss when she grazed it.

She closed her eyes and pictured Slate leaning over her, holding her legs open. But not for his tongue—for his *cock*.

She slid a finger inside. Slate's tongue had stretched her so wide that soon she could fit a second finger and then a third. Wet noises filled the room, so lewd her cheeks burned.

Ruby rubbed that sweet spot he had found so easily with his tongue, her fingers moving faster as she imagined him filling her up.

I have prepared you well, said imaginary Slate, his voice full of scraping rocks. *Look how easily you take my cock, little witch.*

"Yes," Ruby sighed. She reached down to rub at her sensitive clit, both hands faltering as she imagined Slate swelling inside her, his cock jerking as he filled her up.

Take it, said imaginary Slate, forcing his knot inside. *And come for me.*

Ruby tensed and came, her dress rucked up around her hips. Wave after wave of pleasure rolled through her, even as her clit stung with overstimulation.

After, she slid her fingers out and stared at them.

Three small human fingers and nothing more.

They had a lot of preparation to do.

SIX

"Brother," Slate said. "Is this a suitable meal to give to a mortal?"

He held out the rabbit.

Wick stared at it. He raised his fiery eyes to Slate and gave him an incredulous look most others would get killed over.

"*This* is what you summoned me for?" Wick asked.

Slate snorted. He should have never bothered him. But Wick was his only brother who frequented the mortal realm. The only one he spoke to, anyway. Apparently, he had many siblings who roamed the mortal realms, but they were even younger than Wick and more beast than person. Absolutely useless to talk to unless you wanted something to kill.

"Apologies for thinking you would be useful," Slate said.

Wick sighed, his tail drooping. He was easily susceptible to insults, which Slate appreciated about him. Even if it often led to Slate feeling guilty and soothing them before he left.

"I stay away from mortals," Wick said quietly. "Remember?"

"Yes, yes. You and your bleeding heart. Now..." Slate raised the rabbit a second time. "She insisted mortals eat meat. Is this appropriate?"

Wick leaned in and sniffed it. A leaf drifted past his head, a shadow tendril wafting from it to graze his ear.

Wick batted it away distractedly and leaned back. "So, your mortal is still here?"

"You haven't given me an answer," Slate replied.

Wick scratched his horns. "Mortals eat all kinds of things, brother. Last time I was near a town—"

The dog spirit barked merrily in the distance.

Wick's tail twitched. "What was that?"

"Nothing," Slate said.

But Wick's keen eyes were already tracking the dark forest, looking for the source of the noise. The flames inside them flared, and Slate stepped into the space Wick was staring at. He might get annoyed with that insufferable dog spirit, but it was still lost in Slate's void. That meant it was under Slate's protection. He would not allow the spirit to come to harm, especially not from Wick's insatiable blood hunger.

The fire in Wick's eyes spasmed and died.

"Sorry," Wick said, blinking hard. "The last time... yes. The last time I was near mortals, I saw a small one eating dirt."

"Dirt," Slate repeated flatly.

Wick nodded. "Why not send her to the forest and feed her some dirt?"

"She *was* in the forest. She cooked herself eggs."

"Maybe your void's dirt tastes strange to her," Wick suggested.

Slate's tail flicked in irritation. He was starting to suspect that Wick's knowledge of mortals was just as lacking as his own. "Are you honestly saying you don't know any more about mortals than I do?"

"I know things," Wick said defensively. "I just try to stay away, brother. You know why."

Slate snorted dismissively. Wick's blood frenzy had gone on long enough for him to stop feeling guilty over it. *Slate* never felt bad about eating mortals. Why should Wick care if he did it more frequently than most?

Then again, Slate reminded himself that if Wick stopped caring, he would not be one of the only siblings Slate bothered talking to. Wick's determination not to kill unless he had to was endearing, if not bewildering.

It is like you and your void, he told Slate once. *How you don't want to hurt anyone in it. Except the mortal realm is my void since I don't have my own.*

Slate supposed he had to find some way to rationalize it. Being stuck in the mortal realm sounded awful. At least Wick had never known anything different.

Wick sniffed the rabbit again. "So why is this mortal bound to you in the first place? Is this your doing or hers?"

"Hers," Slate said. "Do you think I would allow her to stay in my void if I had a choice?"

He couldn't stomach the idea of sharing his void with *anyone*. Lost souls were guided away as soon as he found them. Paimon had overstayed his welcome more than enough times, and now they hadn't talked in a century. And yet...

Slate huffed, clenching the rabbit's feet so hard the tiny bones cracked. Something about this mortal made him *not* hate having her around. She was irritating, to be sure. But for some reason, he didn't spend all their time together wishing he could go back to sleep. He actually wanted to know more about her. As if it was worth getting to know a mortal who lived... what? A century, at most? He'd taken naps longer than that.

"Paimon has a ward protecting a town in the mortal realm," Slate admitted. "It is failing. She beseeched me to renew it."

"Beseeched," Wick repeated. "You mean she cast a spell on you. What is the issue? Is this why you've been seeking Paimon?"

"Mostly. But since Paimon is nowhere to be found, I can do it. Only..." Slate paused. He did not like to lie. He had no moral qualms with it; it was just tricky to keep track of.

"Paimon crafted it from ancient and powerful magic," he began.

Wick nodded intently. Then the nodding stopped, and Slate sighed as he saw the realization click in his fiery eyes. He had been hoping Wick was young enough not to know about ward magic.

"You must *lie* with her," Wick exclaimed, wings flaring in shock.

"Yes," Slate snapped. "Why do you look so surprised? Many have done it. Haven't you?"

Wick's wings folded up against his back. "I—yes. Of course. I'm just surprised. You are one of the largest Skullstalkers, and she is... *very* small. Even for a mortal."

She is, Slate thought. It was supposed to be an annoyed thought or, at least, grudging. But instead, he felt his cock fill under his loincloth as he remembered his hand wrapping around her small torso, her impossibly tiny hole squeezing around his tongue. Her hand swallowed up by his own. It made his mouth fill with saliva, made him want to eat her up. But it also triggered something unexpected: he wanted to *protect* her. To guard her in ways beyond any lost soul who came into his void. To claim her, drape her in shadows, and show everyone whom she belonged to.

She was bound to him. She *was* his — at least for a little while.

Slate frowned. He was not used to his emotions being so powerful. What was this little witch doing to him?

"That is not the only problem," he announced. "She has never mated before."

Wick made a confused noise in his throat, like embers crackling.

"Really? Why?" Wick frowned. "How old is she?"

Slate had no idea. He had only just found out that mortals didn't even live a single century.

"I should return," he said quickly. "She is hungry. *Again*. Let yourself out."

He turned toward the castle, the rabbit still dangling from his hand.

"Hope she enjoys the rabbit," Wick called after him hopefully. "Rub some dirt on it!"

Slate did not "rub some dirt on it." Instead, he ventured back to the mortal realm to steal a pie off a windowsill after overhearing some local children confess how much they were looking forward to eating it.

Then he returned to his void, feeling more foolish than he had done in a long time. He wished Paimon was here. The goat deity knew more about mortals than all his brothers combined. He actually *talked* to them sometimes. Unlike Wick, who hid from them like his existence depended on it. Which it didn't. The mortals' existence did. None of them had ever come close to taking Wick down, no matter how prepared they were.

He appeared in the bedroom to find her lying on the bed, her hands trailing along her silky black dress.

She startled, her eyes widening as she saw the rabbit and the pie. Her dark hair had dried while he was gone. It was light and cloudy, with a more entrancing curl than before. The firelight reflected off it, streaking her hair with familiar blue.

Slate's mouth watered. Her skin was so flushed and warm. It would be so easy to hold her down and—

You will not eat her, he reminded himself sternly and held out the food. "I hope these will suffice."

He set them down on the bed.

Ruby hesitated, then picked up the rabbit by the scruff.

"I can remove the bones," he offered reluctantly.

Ruby's face twisted in a complicated array of expressions he could not begin to parse.

"No, thank you," she said and paused. "Huh. I might actually take you up on that. But after I skin it, okay?"

"Of course." *Skinning.* He assumed mortals only did that for clothing purposes, not because they couldn't eat fur. What a weak palate.

She picked up the pie. For a moment, it seemed like she would place it on her lap. Then she looked down at the black fabric and hesitated, setting the pie beside her on the coverlet instead.

Slate watched her smooth her dress down as if checking it for crumbs. She had touched it so reverently when she examined her reflection earlier. He thought back to the town he had visited, all those mortals walking around in plain, functional clothes much like the ones she had been wearing when she appeared.

It was fine for those mortals. But Ruby deserved better. As long as she was *his,* anyway.

Ruby turned back to the pie and laughed in shock.

Slate leaned over to examine it. "What is it?"

"Nothing," she said, sweeping her frizzy hair behind her ears. "This is my neighbor's pie. Glenda. I recognize the latticing; she spends ages on it."

Slate tried to translate this into Skullstalker customs. He had never had a neighbor, but he would be annoyed if someone stole from him.

"Is that bad?" he asked.

She raised her head, her dark eyes gleaming in the firelight. "No, this is wonderful! She'll throw a fit. I want to feel bad for her because she has to cook for so many children, but she's such a—"

She cut off with a wince. "Never mind. Witches aren't supposed to badmouth the people they protect."

Slate huffed. "I have never heard of such a rule."

She laughed again. It was choppy and shocked, as most of her laughs had been. As if she hadn't been expecting whatever he said that provoked the laugh. She *had* been expecting him to eat her, after all.

He watched her scoop up a gleaming shred of pie and slot it into her mouth. Pastry crumbled over her palm, fruit slicking her fingers.

"Sorry," she said, muffled through the mouthful. "I'll clean up the crumbs."

"I live in a forest," he reminded her. "Crumbs are the least of my concerns."

He watched her eat. Her cheeks bulged, her lips shining with juice, and he was filled with a hunger that had nothing to do with that pale mortal food. It was beginning to disturb him. He wanted so little until she showed up.

"Mortal," he started. "How old are you?"

She covered her wet mouth. "Twenty-four."

"And how long do mortals live? A century?"

She laughed, coughing with the crumbs. "What? *Eighty*, if we're lucky. I hear stories of people living to see a century over the sea, but folk say all sorts of things about lands they know nothing about."

Twenty-four, Slate thought. If a mortal lived until eighty... that would make Ruby a quarter-way through her life. What a pitifully short amount of time to exist.

An uneasy feeling twisted inside Slate's stomach.

He pressed it down. "How is the food?"

She made a pleased noise, covering her mouth as she chewed another mouthful of pie. Her pink tongue darted out and swirled around her finger, sucking off a streak of fruit.

"I was wondering," she asked.

He tore his gaze away from her sticky finger. "Yes?"

She bit her lip. "Do demons ever come to this realm?"

"Did you see one?" Slate asked, amused by his own joke. If she encountered a demon, she would be dead.

"No," she said hurriedly. "I just wondered."

"Sometimes they sneak in from other realms," Slate admitted. "More often, lost souls corrode and become demons while they are trapped here."

Ruby stopped chewing. She swallowed hard. "*Trapped*? They *become* demons?"

"Yes," Slate said, wondering what they were teaching witches in her part of the mortal realm nowadays. He was sure they used to be more knowledgeable than this. "Lost souls appear here, most often when something goes wrong after their death. Most of them, I can lead to where they must go. But some refuse to follow. Those unfortunate souls turn into shades."

Ruby's eyes went huge and round. "But... the dog spirit..."

"He is..." Slate's tail swished. "A rare case. He does not refuse to follow. I just have nowhere to lead him yet. I am supposed to feel it. But there is nothing."

"Oh." The tension drained from her shoulders, but her expression stayed worried. "It's mostly shades that try to get past the ward barrier at Sweetsguard."

"That doesn't surprise me," he said.

Ruby frowned, tugging at her dress strap absent-mindedly. It had fallen when her shoulders sagged.

Slate watched the loose material and concentrated. His hand folded into a fist, claws pricking his palm.

Ruby gasped and twisted to watch her sleeve. It was turning into a liquid shadow, tightening around her body just as Slate had commanded it.

Slate's fist loosened in his robes. "You startle easily."

"I'm not startled," she said, too fast. She plucked at her new sleeve, which fitted much more snugly. There was some apprehension in her expression. But just as he was about to apologize, her mouth quirked in such wonder all the breath fled from Slate's chest.

"Okay," Ruby said as if to herself. Then she looked up, and her face smoothed out.

She moved the pie and then the dead rabbit to the nightstand, straining to reach its tall height. "We need to... practice. Like you talked about."

Slate's cock thickened under his robes. Yet another

irrational physical sensation he hadn't had to bother with in centuries. But *gods*, did it feel good.

"As you say," he said.

He surged over her, pushing her flat against the bed and trapping her hands above her. The bed was too big for him, and it completely dwarfed the tiny mortal lying on it. It would stand up well to whatever they did to it.

Ruby gasped, a delicious flush spreading down her plunging neckline.

Slate fought the urge to run his tongue down it. Soon, he told himself. Not yet.

He forced his gaze back up to her reddening face. "How would you like to begin?"

"I..." Ruby trailed off. Her teeth dug into her lip, and Slate wondered, for the very first time in his long existence, what kissing a mortal would be like.

Her raven hair fell down her cheek. Her dark eyes glittered in the firelight. Lying here like this, covered with him, she truly did look like she was crafted out of shadows. Like she was *his*.

"How many times will it take?" Ruby asked shyly.

Slate had no clue. But it was not *his* town that would die if they ran out of time.

He nuzzled her cheek, listening to her heartbeat pound under her flimsy skin.

"A pertinent question," Slate said, unsurprised to find his voice was even more gravelly than usual. "Would you like to find out?"

SEVEN

Ruby expected the low growl to frighten her.

Instead, it made the heat between her legs pool even faster. She rubbed her thighs together under her dress, appalled and wondrous. Since when had she been interested in feral beasts? She had never dreamed of monsters when she was alone at night, touching herself in her empty cottage. And here she was, dripping wet at the idea of being ravaged by a *Skullstalker*, of all things.

Then Ruby saw the impossible bulge tenting his loincloth, and the fantasy faded with a pang of fear. Daydreams were all well and good until reality set in. There was a *reason* they were practicing. If he really held her down and had his way with her, she would be screaming before he was even halfway in, and not with ecstasy.

"Little witch," Slate rumbled from where he had her

pinned against the bed. "You did not answer my question."

It took Ruby a moment to remember. His eyes were so intense on hers, his stature so imposing as he leaned over her.

But his grip was gentle. Her wrists didn't even sting, and his claws were the barest brush against her skin.

Ruby shivered, her mind awash with lurid images. Most of them were impossible. They had to start slowly.

She motioned at his face. "Your skull mask... does it come off?"

"No." He ducked down, gliding the sleek bone over her nose. "This is my face. Does it not please you?"

"No, it does," Ruby said hastily. She was shocked to find that it wasn't a lie. Not entirely, anyway. It intimidated her, of course. But there was something about a monster staring down at her with a skull mask leaking shadows that excited her.

Ruby twisted her wrists in his unrelenting grip. "You could... take my dress off?"

Slate cocked his head. At first, she thought he was going to ask her to do it herself.

Then he let go of her wrists—only with one hand, the other keeping her held tight.

That one hand reached down, a sharp claw touching just above her neckline.

He dragged his claw down. The shadowy material parted under his touch, and at first, Ruby thought he was shredding it. But there was no tearing noise, no drag of pressure.

He wasn't tearing it. He was making it *vanish*, Ruby realized, her stomach swooping. He had conjured it out of shadows, and he could make it go away just as easily.

Ruby gasped. The shadows ran down her like water. Her beautiful dress dissipated against the coverlet, and suddenly, she was lying naked below him. She was suddenly glad for the fireplace, which had turned the air from chilly to something she could stand being naked in.

Slate's claw stopped below her navel. His gaze roved over her, and Ruby's face heated as she realized that he could have her naked at any time. One light touch and she could be fully bare and ready for him.

She glanced down at his impossible cock.

Well. Ready for *something*, at least. Not that he seemed incredibly interested in her when she had offered herself at the ward. She still didn't understand it. He *seemed* like he wanted her if that growl was anything to go by. Would he turn her down again if she offered her hand or mouth?

Slate's claw trailed down, curling against the coarse hair over her mound. He was so big he could easily hold her wrists and toy with her hole without straining his arms.

"How many years are you into adulthood?"

Ruby concentrated. It was hard to think with him looming over her like this, his black eyes half-lidded as he slid a finger further and further down. She could feel herself sweating. Her mouth was dry, her heart pounding so loud she could hear it. Could *he* hear it? She hoped not.

"S-six," she stammered. "I was a woman at eighteen."

"Six years," Slate mused. He sounded conflicted. Ruby didn't know if that was because she was young or because he couldn't translate mortal years into immortal ones.

He hummed, the noise oddly birdlike. Much like the birdsong she had heard during her night in the forest. It made her wonder how much he was part of his void and how much his void was part of him.

Then his claw grazed her sensitive clit, and all her thoughts dissolved into too-intense pleasure.

She let out a pained hiss.

"I'm fine," she assured him when he drew back, surprised. "I'm just..."

She bit her lip. She wasn't going to explain how she had gotten herself off on this bed earlier.

"Claws," she explained.

The pressure against her mound went blunt. "So very sensitive."

"I know," she said apologetically. She twisted her wrists in his grip.

"Maybe just focus on preparing me," she told him. "Rather than... other things."

Slate's dark brow furrowed. But he pressed his finger against her folds, rubbing obediently against the entrance.

"You have never mated," he said. "Why?"

"I..." Ruby's mouth dropped open, a moan spilling out as he pressed his fingertip inside. He was so *big*. One of his fingers was easily worth three of hers. She could already feel the strain, even as she started to relax around the intrusion.

"The men in my town aren't appealing," she admitted breathlessly. It was an understatement if she'd ever heard one—calling them *men* was a step too far. *Immature boys* were more like it. Ruby had avoided them when they were growing up, and she avoided them now. It was one of the good parts of her isolation: she didn't have to put up with them leering at her in the market anymore. Instead, they avoided her or shot her suspicious looks when she passed. And, of course, they showed up shame-faced and mumbling when they needed their cock sores healed after they got back from visiting the city.

"Understandable," Slate said, working a finger against her sweet spot. "Most humans aren't."

Ruby assured herself she wasn't offended. But she couldn't ignore the shard of ice in her heart that appeared at the words.

He let her wrists go and started cupping her breast. His thumb was huge, at least twice the size of the nipple he brushed over, and Ruby arched into it with a conflicted moan.

She couldn't help it. She needed to ask.

"But I am?" She tried to pair it with a coy smile, but she was never good at coy. It came out shy and vulnerable instead, so meek it would have made her wince if he wasn't fluttering his giant finger against that spot that made her see stars.

"You are..." Slate hesitated. "Not unappealing. For a mortal."

With that, he tucked a second finger inside her.

Ruby bit her cheek. The stretch stung, but the slide was delicious. She was so wet his fingers squelched inside her.

She waited for the sting to subside. The pleasure was already mounting, overtaking it until the pain was a distant pinprick.

"Can you take another?" Slate asked, his voice more rumble than words.

Ruby cringed. "I... I don't think so."

The fireplace pulsed, sending up a shockingly tall gout of flame. It lit him from behind, haloing him in blue light.

"I think you can," he said softly.

Ruby doubted it. Then he curled his fingers inside her, and those doubts were suddenly hazy and far away.

"O-okay," she gasped.

Slate huffed against her hair. A third finger nudged against her entrance.

Ruby braced herself. But the stretch was too much. Even when his gentle probing turned insistent, that third fingertip was nowhere close to sliding in with the others.

"It won't fit," Ruby blurted. "Stop."

Slate stilled. A low chirp rumbled in his chest, and Ruby's knees trembled against the bed as failure thrummed through her. She could hardly take two fingers. How was she ever going to take his knot?

She glanced up at him, eyes filling with nervous tears. Was he disappointed? Was now where everything turned, and he started to act like she had expected him to when she appeared in his void?

But the words Slate spoke were not of disappointment. If anything, he sounded fascinated as he pressed his two fingers deep inside her.

"You really are incredibly small," he said roughly. "I keep forgetting. Even when I am looking at you, it seems impossible anyone should be so small. Even a mortal woman."

His fingers twisted inside her. Ruby moaned, her grip tightening on his elbows.

"I'm not *that* small," she insisted. "I'm... perfectly normal for a human."

"Yes," Slate said. "Still."

The implication made Ruby shiver: he was so very *in*human. This was a Skullstalker who didn't even realize how long humans lived. He was entirely unknown, and she was letting him push his big fingers inside her, deeper than anyone had ever been.

The heat in her core was building. Ruby dropped her head against his massive arm. Slate's fingering slowed, and Ruby wondered if she had done something he disliked.

"Sorry," she said, lifting her head.

He cut her off. "Are you going to come like this? Just from my fingers inside?"

Ruby's sensitive clit throbbed. She thought about touching it, but just the idea made her wince. She'd never used it so much before.

"Yes," she admitted. Then his fingers crooked, and she groaned. "*Yes.*"

Slate continued to make a beckoning motion inside her, fluttering against that spot that made her hips buck against him. Then his fingers parted, and Ruby whimpered.

He's stretching me, she realized. *Getting me ready.*

That was what all this was about, after all. Preparing her to take his cock.

She cried out and came, clenching around his fingers. She could hear herself making pitiful noises, but it was difficult to care when she felt so good. Her hips flowed against him, riding out every last wave of pleasure until she was spent and quaking.

And still, Slate's fingers remained.

She lifted her head off his arm. She was damp with sweat, her hair a frizzy mess where she'd rubbed them against him.

Ruby grimaced as she noticed she had left a patch of sweat on his skin. She was *small*, sure, but she was also so many other things he wasn't used to. Including dripping... on him.

She smoothed a self-conscious hand through her messy hair. "That was... thank you."

Ruby didn't know if it was the right thing to say. But Slate nodded, his fingers sliding out of her with a slick pop that made her throb with emptiness.

He moved from the bed to stand before it. Ruby's eyes fell to his stiff cock under his loincloth. He was at the perfect height. If she just leaned up, she could mouth at the fabric.

She bit her lip, waiting. Surely now, he would ask. He didn't ask last time, but *surely*—

"I will leave you to your rest," he announced.

Slate turned toward the door. Ruby watched despairing as his cock vanished from view, still heavy under his loincloth.

"Wait," Ruby blurted.

Slate turned. She was shocked and dismayed to see the bulge was already going down. Did he only do it for her benefit?

"I..." Ruby eyed the wilting bulge cautiously. "I want to make you come."

Slate made another trilling noise deep in his throat. "It is not necessary."

Apparently not, Ruby thought as she watched the bulge continue to shrink. She wanted to back down, apologize for the smear of sweat on his skin, and try to find that bathroom again.

But she *wanted* it. And she hoped he wanted it, too. Not to mention it was the least she could do after how good he'd been to her.

"I know," she said. "I just... if you don't want to, that's fine."

Slate's tail flicked behind him in a way that reminded Ruby of an anxious animal. Then he stepped toward her, and the flick turned to a swish. Less anxious animal, more stalking tiger.

He loomed over her. His lips parted, and Ruby

wondered if those fangs would nick her if he kissed her. He still hadn't kissed her yet, and she didn't know if she should be expecting it. Those fangs looked dangerously sharp.

Slate pushed her into the bed.

Ruby let out a squeak. Slate's hand was splayed over her torso, so huge she couldn't help remembering when she was sprawled over the ward stone. His hand had wrapped around her middle with such little effort. He could move her however he wanted, and she would be powerless to stop it.

It should have been horrifying. But the fear was getting smaller every time she spoke to him. Even lying helpless under his massive hand, the most she could muster was a cold tingle at the back of her neck. And it faded quickly as the hand trailed up to cup her breast once more.

He was watching her with that same intensity as always, but now there was a layer of curiosity under it.

He's deciding what to do with me, Ruby thought. It was enough to make her poor clit stiffen once more, her hole throbbing around nothing.

Slate said, his voice low and silky, "I want your mouth."

Ruby's jaw ached at the thought of fitting around his bulge, which was hardening again under his loincloth.

"I can't fit..." she trailed off, embarrassed.

"I know," he consoled her. "You do not need to put it inside. You can use your lips. Your tongue. You can still suck."

He unknotted his loincloth. Shadows wisped around his groin before dissipating into the warm air.

Ruby sat up and stared. He had been naked in the clearing, but she had been so nervous she didn't get to appreciate it. Then he had been kneeling, and she was too busy thrashing on his tongue to pay much attention.

He was magnificent. Pale and strange, to be sure, but magnificent. His alabaster skin made her want to run her tongue over it. She wanted to wrap her hands around his curling horns. To have that swishing tail curl around her leg and squeeze.

And his cock...

Ruby's mouth watered. She shuffled forward until she was sitting in front of it, her mouth inches away.

It was as intimidatingly large as she remembered. There was a rosy flush to the tip, which was new. Or maybe she'd been so busy staring at his knot in excited horror that she hadn't noticed it last time.

"My tongue is only human-sized," she said apologetically.

Slate laughed. It sounded like river stones dragging over boulders. "I would expect nothing more."

"I'm just telling you," she said. "So you don't expect... I mean to say, I'm..."

Slate touched her chin. The touch was so soft Ruby's words died in her throat.

"I am fully aware you are human," he told her, sounding amused rather than annoyed as she feared. "You don't need to warn me. Now, begin."

Ruby let out an involuntary laugh. She gripped the

base of his cock experimentally, just above the knot. Her fingers didn't even fit around it. Never mind the knot resting below her grip.

She gave it an experimental stroke. It kicked in her hand, and she gaped as pearly liquid beaded at the tip.

"Mortal," Slate said. "I asked for your mouth."

"Right," she said hurriedly. After a moment of panic that reminded her of the second before she started a spell she had never tried before, she pressed her open mouth against his cockhead.

It was... shockingly soft. Like velvet. It was also very cool, which she doubted was normal. There was a faint taste of salt, and when she moved her lips toward the center, the taste got stronger.

She licked hesitantly at the slit. Salt burst over her tongue, and she muffled a moan as a second bead of pearly liquid fed right into her mouth.

She suckled again. Another burst of salt. Her mouth pooled with saliva as she sucked harder, massaging the massive length with her hands.

Slate grunted. He sounded shocked, and Ruby hoped it wasn't because she was bad at this.

She pulled back, considering. Then she stretched her mouth as wide as she could and tried to fit it around the head.

Nowhere close. But Slate's hips hitched, and even though it did nothing but force her off, Ruby was pleased to see a chink in his self-control. The most she had seen him lose it was when he was gripping her knees and moaning as she fucked his tongue inside her.

She paused, remembering the blissful vibrations his moans had created against her. Then she attached her lips to his cockhead and let out a cautious moan.

Slate grabbed her hair with a moan. She couldn't see how the moan could have caused any true vibrations, but she supposed he liked her noises. Back in the clearing, he had gripped her thighs harder the more she moaned.

She ran her tongue down his cool shaft, following a vein the same thickness as her pinkie. All the way down until she reached his knot. Then, after some consideration, she pressed her lips around the ridge of his knot and sucked.

"*Ah.*" Slate's head tipped back. The shadows wafting from his skull mask flexed. His claw stroked absentmindedly against her scalp, and Ruby shivered as she realized his palm could envelop her entire head easily.

He could make me do anything, she thought, and the words were a heady pulse between her legs. *And still, he is only giving me what I can take.*

Ruby licked and sucked, her hands moving over his cockhead now as she worked his knot. She could feel it swelling against her lips, velvety smooth hardness bulging bigger and bigger—

"Mortal," Slate repeated, strained. He tugged gently on her hair. "Lie back."

Ruby pulled away, confused. "What?"

But before she could worry that she was doing a bad job, he pushed her flat on her back and held her there. His other hand reached to grip his cock, stroking it so fast his hand blurred.

"Oh," Ruby said weakly. She craned her head to watch and was rewarded by a line of come splashing over her chin. The next rope hit her breasts, her belly, dripping over the hand he was using to hold her there.

That, at least, was warm. Ruby's tongue darted out to taste it as Slate wrung the last few drops out. It was so salty she thought she should be disgusted. But she couldn't stop herself from licking another taste off her cheek.

Finally, Slate sagged. His cock softened against his hand. But as he let go, Ruby saw it—his knot was still huge and hard underneath.

Ruby's mouth filled with saliva once more. She imagined him pumping into her, filling her up again and again as she lay over the ward stone, limp and drooling.

Slate straightened. There was no sweat on his skin, and his chest had already stopped heaving. He lifted his hand, and before he had finished flicking it, his loincloth was back in place. The shadows around his skull mask stilled, and he was the impassive Bygone once again. Calm. In control. Untouchable.

He looked down at her, flushed and covered in come. For a moment, she thought he would say something.

Then he stepped back, bowing his head. "I will leave you to rest."

"Wait," she blurted.

He stopped. Of course, he did. For all he held her down, he stopped when she asked.

Ruby sat up, his come sliding off her torso and onto

the coverlet. She winced. She would have to clean that before she could sleep.

"Do you really think we can do this?" she asked uncertainly. "Make it fit, I mean."

"My brother assured me it is possible." Slate paused. His claws twitched at his side. Then he reached out, and Ruby's heart thumped as she waited for his hands on her skin again.

But it didn't come. Slate waved his palm over her come-covered torso, and all evidence of their time together vanished. Her dress wove into existence over her skin, shadows solidifying into the dress she had been wearing before he came in.

Ruby touched her plunging neckline, which was now only damp with sweat. She was happy to be clean and clothed again, of course. But some part of her was upset, and she didn't know why.

"Rest, little witch," Slate told her. He turned to leave.

Ruby rubbed her sweaty skin, trying to shake off the stubborn feeling of loss. He had done something *nice*. So what if he hadn't bothered to touch her?

"Ruby," she called.

Slate paused at the door. He didn't say anything, but his head tilted her way. Waiting.

"I like it when you call me Ruby," she explained timidly.

Slate didn't move. His bone mask glinted in the firelight.

"Rest," he said. "Ruby."

EIGHT

The mortal realm smelled like dirt.

Slate still had not asked Ruby whether she ate dirt. But judging by the amount of effort the Glenda woman was putting into making a second pie when she had mounds of dirt in her garden, he assumed that it was not, in fact, a crucial part of a mortal's diet.

He lingered in the corner of her kitchen, concentrating on the invisibility spell. It had been a long time since he had needed it, and he couldn't afford to lose it now. Not when he was so close to finding out a mortal food that wasn't pie or rabbit.

He caught glimpses every time she stormed over to the cupboard, grumbling as she went.

"Lousy, greedy, good for nothings," Glenda growled as she worked. "Supposed to be able to leave a pie on your own damn windowsill without it getting pinched. Void take them."

She swung open the cupboard again. Slate peered

into it, catching a glimpse of woven bags filled with grains, granules, and flour.

He sighed. He needed more than ingredients—he needed a prepared *meal*. He hadn't even gotten the rabbit right. Ruby didn't only need to skin it but gut and cook it. So many steps before they could eat. Slate had lived millennia with a simple diet: he saw something, he ate it. If necessary, he picked fur out of his teeth afterward. His castle did have a kitchen, but he never used it. That was for whoever was in his void before him, who presumably had a more complicated diet.

Four children of varying ages sprinted into the kitchen, chasing each other with such enthusiasm that Slate felt weary.

"Oi," Glenda snapped, waving a sticky wooden spoon at them. "Calm down, or nobody gets any pie!"

"Okay, Ma," the children trilled in one. None of them slowed down. The smallest one fell close to where Slate was hiding invisibly, and Slate pulled away reflexively. The child had sticky fingers.

The child squinted up at him. For a moment, Slate thought his enchantment had slipped, and he was about to get found out. But the child only stared up at him with a vacant expression, then whirled around.

"MA," he yelled. "CAN I HAVE A CHOCOLATE?"

"Not yet," Glenda said, ducking around the other children on her way to the pie sitting on top of the heating oven. Then she froze, stabbing her wooden spoon at the children standing on top of each other to reach the highest shelves of the cupboard. "Oi! What did I just say?"

"Sorry, Ma," the children chorused.

Glenda sighed, rubbing her lined forehead. "Get out of my sight until dinnertime, alright? Give my poor heart a break."

Slate watched the children tumble out of the room. Then he snuck into the cupboard and took the item the children had been climbing on top of each other to retrieve: a small, brown bar wrapped in smudged cloth.

He was almost out of the house when a young woman leaned her head into the kitchen door. "Glenda! Any word on our witch yet?"

"No, and let's hope it stays that way," Glenda barked.

Slate stopped. There was only one witch that they could be talking about. He stepped back into the house, the chocolate safely cocooned in his cool fingers.

"Aw, don't be like that," the other woman said. "She wasn't all bad. Hoity-toity, but not all bad."

Hoity-toity. Slate did not know the meaning, but it was not said in a complimentary tone. Were witches not revered in the mortal realm anymore? When he and Paimon used to visit, they were held in high esteem. Then again, that was long ago. So long that they had invented a new title for him, and nobody remembered a time when he was named anything else.

Glenda huffed, dropping another strip of pastry over the pie. "You're only saying that because she keeps quiet about your boils."

"I'm sure I don't know what you're talking about,"

the other woman said with a tight smile. "Alright, I might not have liked the girl. But you'd do well to remember that if that Skullstalker ate her, we'd need to find some other witch to hide out in that strange little house on the edge of town. What if the next one's a blabbermouth?"

"Then you'll need to learn how to deal with your own boils," Glenda said distractedly. She knelt to fan the oven flames, then slid the pie inside. "And don't talk about him. You know what happens."

The other woman laughed, exposing several missing teeth. "You suspicious old thing. I'll say his name however much I want! *Bygone, Bygone, Bygone—*"

Glenda straightened, slamming the oven door shut with a sharp bang. "Tessa! Step away from my house, turn around three times, and spit!"

Tessa laughed louder. "Oh, come on."

Glenda waved hurriedly at her.

Slate watched, baffled, as Tessa stepped away from the house and started spinning in place. It seemed like some rudimentary warding ritual... to keep *him* away. Why did they think some spinning and saliva would keep him out?

Slate glided out of the house, still puzzled. The mortals didn't know his name anymore, and they invented strange, false rituals to ward him off. He never had much to do with the mortal realm in the first place, but he was a guide, not a thief. What use would he have with stolen mortal souls?

He had better things to do than venture into the mortal realm, anyway. He had his forest. His nest. Once his deal with Ruby was complete, he would go back to that simple life. Slumbering peacefully, talking to no one, ignoring his brothers' occasional attempts at socializing.

Existence would return to normal. And Ruby would wither and die in the mortal realm, as she should.

Something snapped in his hand.

He opened his fingers. The chocolate was in two pieces. He hadn't noticed he was holding it so tightly.

Ruby was not in the bedroom where he had left her. Nor was she waiting in the anointing room or wandering the long, crumbling hallways.

He closed his eyes and concentrated. He could feel Ruby's presence in his void—partly because she was not meant to be here, partly because of the binding she had placed on him. She was a spot of light in the dark, easily visible from anywhere in his void.

He walked outside to the forest.

Ruby was just beyond the tree line. The dog spirit sat at her side, tail wagging as it watched the mortal step deeper into the forest.

"You must be confused," she was saying to... a lost soul?

Slate blinked. He hadn't felt a soul enter his void. Why hadn't he sensed it?

The lost soul was slumped, filled with murky grey. Its face was flickering, and Slate fought down an uncharacteristic stab of guilt. The soul had clearly been lost for a long time.

The soul lifted its head with a mournful groan.

"...don't know... got here," it croaked.

"Of course," said Ruby soothingly. "What was the last thing you remember?"

The soul moaned. It was a dead human, like many lost souls who stumbled into his void.

"Deidre," it whispered. "I... want... Deidre."

"I'm going to help you find her," Ruby promised.

Her tone made Slate pause. She sounded like she truly meant it. She had already pledged herself to a Skull-stalker to help her town, and now she was pledging to help this soul she had never met.

Slate hummed to make himself known. It was a soft burr, meant to alert without panic.

It didn't work. Ruby shrieked, spinning around. Her hand touched where her knife had lived in her old clothes.

"Oh," she said once she spotted him. Her hand moved against the slick dress fabric, which had no pockets. "Hello. Are you... here to help?"

"It is my job," Slate said. "Step aside."

The dog spirit barked excitedly.

"You too," Slate said.

The dog spirit bumped disobediently into his leg. Slate pushed down a wave of unwanted fondness and allowed the dog spirit just one scratch behind the ears before turning to the lost soul.

It was beginning to have facial features again. Talking often helped them remember who they were before they came here.

"Soul," Slate greeted. "You had unfinished business before you died."

"Deidre," it croaked. "My... love..."

Slate's eyes glowed behind his skull mask as he looked inside the soul's heart. It was connected to Deidre, who was easy enough to find. But the connection was thick and thorny and broke when he attempted to reach into Deidre's dead heart. He caught glimpses of fire and blood and mortals screaming.

"I know where your love is," Slate said. "But you are not going there."

Ruby startled. "What?"

Slate flicked his hand. The lost soul dissipated with a sorrowful cry.

Ruby gasped, whirling on him. "Where did you send him?"

"Tormentum," Slate replied.

Ruby gaped. "The *suffering* void? Why? He wanted to go with Deidre!"

"Deidre would not be happy to see him," Slate explained. "I saw his heart. And I caught glimpses of hers. He slayed her after she laid with another. Her family slayed him in return. They bound him to the suffering void. Where someone wants to be and where they must be do not always match."

"Oh. I thought..." Ruby wilted, confused.

The dog spirit nudged her hand. She petted him distractedly, but the troubled look did not fade.

Slate's hand curled around the chocolate, careful not to clench too hard this time.

"You were doing well," he offered. "Lost souls rarely recognize anyone, let alone a living soul. How did you get him to listen?"

Ruby frowned. "Many people don't want to speak to a witch. You must find a way to make them, or you can never help."

Not for the first time since he met Ruby, Slate was in the surprising position of admiring a mortal. From his limited experience with them, they seemed nasty and brutish, clamoring to grab whatever they could despite their short, meaningless lives.

Ruby stood apart from that. Even when talking to a lost soul she had never met. Even when helping a town who didn't want to speak to her. She had been prepared to give her *life*.

It was a shame she would be gone from this world so fast. The mortal realm needed more like her.

"How could you tell?" Ruby asked. "About Deidre?"

"I read his heart. It is something I can do with lost souls in my void."

Ruby's eyes widened. "Can you read *my* heart?"

Slate huffed a laugh. "You are not lost. You are not part of my void."

"Oh."

Slate expected her to look relieved. But Ruby looked almost disappointed as she absorbed this information, fiddling with her dress.

Slate cleared his throat. "I—"

"Why does the light never change?" Ruby asked. Then she winced. "Sorry, what were you saying?"

He tucked the chocolate into his loincloth. "Never mind. You were asking about the light?"

Ruby nodded, pointing up at the sky. "It's always evening."

Slate looked up at the familiar purples and blacks, trying to remember the last time it had looked different. He couldn't. Was he really getting so ignorant about his own void? Not noticing lost souls, not even noticing the light changing...

"I hadn't noticed," he said honestly.

He reached into his sleeve again. But before he could grip the chocolate, he heard himself ask, "What does *hoity toity* mean?"

Ruby's full mouth twitched.

"Stuck up," she said flatly. "Conceited. Why?"

"No reason." Slate gave her what he hoped was a reassuring smile. It felt odd. He did not smile often, and it seemed to alarm her.

Probably the fangs, Slate thought grumpily. He dropped the smile.

"I visited the mortal realm," he began, pulling the chocolate from his sleeve. "And I found—"

A rustle in the bushes made him stop.

Something twisted inside him, sharp and warning. He had not noticed the lost soul. And he hadn't noticed *this*—not until it was too late.

"Get back," he hissed.

He pushed the chocolate back into his sleeve and swept Ruby behind him, ignoring her gasp as he turned to face the threat.

"What's happening?" Ruby whispered behind him. "I can help."

The dog spirit barked, hackles going up.

Slate shushed them both, the noise thick and chafing in ways he didn't intend. He couldn't help it: something prickled in his throat whenever he encountered one of these things.

"Out," he bellowed. "I see you."

A low snarl echoed through the trees.

Behind him, Ruby shivered. Her heartbeat sped up, making Slate's mouth water. But his hunger was an afterthought. He was full of protective rage, the likes of which he had never experienced. If he hadn't been here...

"*Out*," he growled. "I command you."

Another wild snarl. This one tapered into a howl as the shade demon leaped from the bushes, claws bared.

NINE

Ruby cried out a warning as Slate caught the shade demon by its throat.

"Watch out," she yelled, heart pounding painfully in her chest.

But the demon's claws had already struck true. Black shadows dripped from the cut on Slate's exposed chin. But he didn't make any sound of pain. He only held the shade demon further away, head twisted to avoid its slashing claws.

The dog spirit barked, ready to spring.

"Stay back," Slate commanded.

Ruby caught the dog spirit by its scruff. It squirmed, whining worriedly as Slate held the demon back.

The shade was bigger up close. Ruby had only seen flashes when the last witch of Sweetsguard took her to see the ward borders: the hint of a forked tail, the sparkle of hollow eyes.

This thing was even bigger than her. It looked like a

man stretched to unnatural lengths, his joints twisting and gnarled. Its skin stretched horribly over its bones and its eyes were sunken and black.

The shade demon roared, swiping again at the blood on Slate's face.

Slate's grip tightened.

At first, Ruby thought it wouldn't do anything. Demons didn't need to breathe, after all. But Slade's huge hand got tighter and tighter, the shade's growls quietening until they were nothing more than short, choked noises.

Then the snapping started. First the demon's neck, its head bending at an unnatural angle. Black goo poured out over Slate's hand, thick and oily.

Slate squeezed harder. The cracks spread over the shade demon's body, climbing its face and limbs until it was more cracks than skin.

"Off with you," Slate growled.

He gave one last squeeze. The shade demon splintered into dust, drifting away on the breeze.

Slate shook his hand free of oil.

"Did..." Ruby swallowed. "Where did you send him?"

"Nowhere," Slate replied darkly. "I destroyed him."

Ruby shivered. She had never seen him so imposing. It should have horrified her. But it was hard to be too scared of a monster who just saved her life.

"You're hurt," she whispered.

He let out a low, annoyed growl. "I am fine."

He smoothed a thumb over his bloody chin. The cut kept bleeding.

"See?" he said uselessly. "Fine."

Ruby winced. She didn't know if Skullstalkers needed the same wound care as mortals, but she couldn't leave it without checking it over first.

"Bend down," she told him.

Slate blinked. Ruby panicked and tried to remember if she'd ever given him an instruction before.

"I just want to check it," she tried.

"You needn't," Slate said. And yet he was already kneeling, eyeing her warily as if she could do anything to him with her mortal hands.

Ruby took his chin and turned it carefully. She grabbed her dress hem and dabbed at the wound until she could see into the cut.

She sighed with relief. "Not as deep as I feared. You'll live."

It was what she always said when people came to her Sweetsguard cottage with medical problems, but it made Slate laugh.

"It will take more than a *shade demon* to destroy me," he said, mouth twisting like she had insulted him. "I have killed thousands with little effort."

The dog spirit barked and trotted up to him, curling around his leg.

Slate growled. But for the first time, Ruby spotted a hint of genuine fondness in his black eyes toward the spirit.

"Do not try to get involved again," he told the dog

spirit. "You are small and puny. I will take care of anything that tries to hurt us."

The dog barked and licked his chin.

"Cease," Slate muttered. But he was smiling. Just a little, enough to pull the skin under Ruby's hand.

Only then did Ruby realize she was still touching him. She dropped her dress hastily, letting the bloody material fall around her feet.

Slate straightened and watched the shadows settle. "Now you have blood on your dress."

"I've had worse," Ruby tried. She started to say she would clean it in one of the many bathrooms she had found after she awoke, but Slate was already raising his hand.

He curled a claw. The bloodstain lifted into the air and dissipated.

Ruby rubbed the material in wonder. He could clear his come *and* his blood with a gesture. Was it bad she was disappointed? She liked being marked by him. In some strange, primal way, it made her feel wanted.

"There," Slate said roughly. "Better."

He twisted to survey the forest. Ruby did the same, wishing that she had been able to find the anointing room where she had left her old clothes. Her dagger was with them.

"Was that a lost soul who turned?" she asked, stroking the dog spirit as it trotted back to her. "Like you talked about?"

"Yes. Most of them sneak in from nearby realms,

but..." Slate looked through the endless trees, shadows trailing off the leaves. He looked like he was going to say more, but then his jaw clicked shut beneath his skull mask.

"Never you mind," he said.

He looked troubled. Ruby had a useless urge to touch his arm in comfort. As if she could comfort a Skullskalker, a being who had been alive before her ancestors came to Sweetsguard. She was a speck to him.

She tugged nervously at her dress. "Thank you for protecting me. I don't want to imagine what would've happened if you weren't there."

Slate made a noise in the back of his throat, low and guttural. Then he coughed.

"Well, I was. So... let's not imagine."

Ruby hesitated. "I want my dagger back. In case something like this happens again."

Slate curled his fingers. A dagger appeared in his hand, curved and gleaming black. He held it out.

"Here," he said. "Take it."

She took it, marveling at the sleek blade. It looked obsidian, though she supposed it was just a shadow. The same as her dress and his loincloth.

She bit her lip. "It's beautiful. But I don't have anywhere to put it."

Something clenched around her thigh, and Ruby gasped.

She pulled the dress open at the leg slit. There was a holster band around her inner thigh, just the right size for the newly conjured dagger to fit into.

"Thank you," she said. She stroked the dagger wondrously, marveling at the smooth texture.

She reached to place it into her holster band. Then she paused, heart racing.

She held the dagger out, proud to see her hands were steady. "Would you put it on for me?"

She waited for him to repeat that he needed to sleep, to go scouting through his void; he didn't have time to perform useless tasks for some puny human.

Then he sank to his knees on the forest floor. He did it so slowly, so intently that Ruby's throat went dry.

He plucked the knife out of her hand. "Your leg."

She extended it out of the slit in her dress. She was sure he could feel her trembling as he took her thigh in one huge hand and slid the black dagger into it. The metal was cool against her skin, just like everything else about him.

Ruby looked at his mouth, half-hidden at the spot where the mask ended. They were almost the same height when he kneeled. Close enough to lean in for a kiss.

The dog spirit whined loudly next to them.

Ruby startled. She had forgotten it was there. "Gods. You scared me."

The dog spirit licked her hand apologetically.

Ruby pulled her leg back under her dress, trying to ignore the feel of the dagger against her thigh as she shifted. "You—you were saying something. Before it attacked us."

Slate paused. He was still kneeling, his gaze stuck on her leg as it slipped back under her dress.

"Yes," he said, standing so fast Ruby's head swooped as if she was falling.

He reached for his sleeve. "I—"

"Why didn't it attack me?" Ruby wondered aloud, unable to stop it. "I'm obviously weaker. Why go for a Skullstalker instead? Gods, sorry, I cut you off again."

Slate's hand dropped from his sleeve. "I don't know. Perhaps he only showed up once I arrived."

Something wasn't right. Ruby looked over at the nightstand the dog spirit had led her to. That sketch of Slate and Paimon covered in blood holding a demon's head aloft would still be there, waiting.

"Have you killed a lot of demons?" Ruby asked cautiously.

"I have."

"With... Paimon?"

Slate hesitated. "There were more, once. When things were less settled. Everyone and everything was vying for more territory. Paimon was a shield brother. It was how we met."

Ruby's mind raced with questions. Sweetsguard suddenly felt laughably small and quaint, full of people stumbling around in the dark. She thought she knew Paimon's story, she thought she knew what the Bygone was, and she thought she knew what demons were. She thought she knew her own damn magic. And she was wrong about all of it. It was time to start uncovering the truth.

"Do you think one of them might have done something to Paimon?" she asked.

Slate let out another gruff laugh. "No demon has the power to hurt him. Paimon is not a powerful god, but he is still a god."

"Tell me more about him."

"Paimon is..." Slate looked away, and Ruby tried to imagine how long he had been alive. How many years he had known Paimon. How much he had seen and done and experienced, generations before Ruby was even an idea in her parents' eyes.

"He is kind," he said slowly. "And cocky. He was always exploring the realms. He tried to get me to join him. He stopped trying, some time ago. He also stopped exploring."

He paused. "He was one of the only non-mortals I ever met who enjoyed the mortal realm."

"He did?"

Slate inclined his head. "He was human, once. A long time ago. He said he enjoyed watching your realm because it reminded him what it was like."

Ruby wanted to cry. She knew none of this. How did she know so little of her own god? She had prayed to him her whole life. She thought she heard him answer, sometimes. Nothing direct—a glow of pride when she cast a successful spell or comfort when she asked for it.

She swallowed a sudden lump in her throat. "Did he ever watch his followers? Did he come to Sweetsguard?"

"He was devoted to his followers. I'm sure he did watch you."

Ruby laughed wetly. She wiped a tear away, embarrassed.

"Oh," said Slate stiffly. "You are weeping again."

"It's not bad!" Ruby swiped her cheeks, fighting back a sob. "I'm just—I'm so relieved. He gives me magic, but I always hoped he—I don't know—that he cared. About me."

She rubbed her chest, trying to soothe the ache in her ribcage. There were times after the last witch of Sweetsguard died when Paimon was the only person she spoke to all day. Knowing he not only heard her but might have really sent some of that comfort she thought she felt, it was like balm on an old wound.

"Thank you," she whispered. "For telling me."

Slate nodded. His hands clenched and loosened at his sides, his tail swishing.

Nervous, Ruby realized, astounded. *I think he's nervous.*

"I will continue my search to discover what has become of him," Slate said. "Until then... do you wish to practice again?"

Ruby giggled, smearing tears off her cheeks. The request made her clit throb painfully. She had stuffed herself with her fingers before she slept last night, or whatever passed for night in this unchanging place, and she had winced the whole way through.

"I would," she said. "But I'm... I'm quite sore."

Slate frowned.

"No, it's fine! I'm just not used to it." Ruby bit her lip, rubbing her thighs together carefully to feel the flat of the dagger he had strapped to her thigh. A dress made of shadows and now a dagger, it made her think of being covered in his come. *Marked* by him, in whatever manner he saw fit.

"Tomorrow," she said. "We can try again tomorrow."

Slate nodded. "Then I will take my leave. My nest is calling."

Ruby jumped in front of him before he could vanish through the trees.

"Wait," she pleaded. "I'm... I'm always lost. Could you show me around? I never know where I'm going."

"You needn't know," he said. "We are bound. I will take you wherever you need."

He started to step around her. She leaped in front again, heart racing with her audacity.

"But when you go away," she tried. "When you sleep, I still want to know. Just while I'm here. Please?"

She gave him her best smile. Then—with a wild hope that bordered on insanity—she toyed with her neckline, pressing a finger under the shadowy fabric.

Slate's eyes did not drop to follow it. But he did sound unnecessarily distracted when he said, "Follow me."

TEN

Skullstalkers were not a nervous species.

Slate reminded himself of this fact as he led Ruby into his nest.

Skullstalkers were one of the most dangerous creatures in any realm. They rarely had reasons to be anxious, especially one as old and powerful as Slate.

So, there was no reason for the shadows around his skull mask to start billowing like a storm.

Ruby tore her eyes away from the nest to watch the shadows pour. "Is that meant to happen?"

"Yes," Slate assured her. "Completely normal."

He clenched his fists at his sides, willing the shadows to be still. It was no use. There was an old animal instinct arising in him, hissing and feral. It reminded him of his earliest days when he didn't know what a castle was, and his bone mask was a thin membrane his brothers could pierce with one claw.

There was a cave. He was almost certain. One of his brothers—he couldn't remember which one—had brought in someone who wasn't supposed to be there. And the air had gone thick with the same fearful, protective scent spilling off of Slate right now: *danger*, it warned. *Intruder, fight, kill!*

Slate assured the instinct that there would be no killing. Certainly not Ruby, who was gazing around the nest with such sweet wonder it made the instinct die down to a low hiss.

"It looks so soft," she said. "I didn't notice before."

She took a step toward it, then hesitated. She looked back toward him for permission.

Slate opened his mouth to say she could look but not touch. He had not allowed anyone to touch his nest, even Paimon. Except for the dog spirit, who had done it while he was sleeping. The little bastard.

"Go ahead," he said instead.

Ruby's surprised smile was almost worth how annoyed he was at himself. He was one of the most powerful creatures in the voids. And he was letting some puny mortal touch his nest, getting her scent all over it. Not only that, he was fetching her food and spinning her dresses and daggers out of shadows. What was happening to him?

"This part of the forest is protected," Slate told her as she pressed at the fur lining the nest. "Just like the castle. If I am away, I am either fetching something for you in the mortal realm or I am here."

Ruby looked over. One of her feet was in the nest, bracing to haul herself up.

"Will I have to try very hard to wake you?"

Slate considered. "We are bound. So, no. I will sense you."

Ruby didn't bring up that he wasn't able to sense that demon before until it was on top of them. Or the lost soul until she had started talking to it. But he could see it in her face as she looked away, climbing into the nest on her hands and knees.

She settled into the middle of the nest, feeling the soft surface with a growing grin.

"I didn't think it would be so *comfortable*," she gushed. She ran the fur between her fingers. "Is this deer velvet?"

"I don't know what that is," Slate said honestly. "It is Helvik fur. A creature that dwells in a long-forgotten void," he explained when she gave him a blank look.

"Well, it's lovely." Ruby ran her hands once more over the fur, then touched a feather next to her head. It was from a bird in his own void, and he thought she would recoil from the shadows dripping off of it. But her smile stayed bright and vibrant, her eyes softening in awe as she stroked his nest.

Then her stomach rumbled. She winced, her gaze flying to him nervously.

Slate stepped forward. "Are you hungry?"

"I have pie in my room," Ruby said hastily and paused. "*The* room. There's a lot of it left; I will be fine for today."

Slate couldn't tell if she was lying. He still didn't know how much mortals needed to eat. But if she was hungry now…

He reached into his loincloth and brought out the wrapped bar of chocolate.

"It was in a human kitchen," he explained. "I assume it is suitable."

He held it out. Ruby took it, her small fingers brushing his.

"Wow," she said quietly.

She was holding it so reverently that Slate frowned. "Is it not part of your diet? You said—"

"No, it's wonderful!" Ruby clasped it to her chest as if he would take it away from her. "We have no chocolatiers in town. There is one person who sells it on market day. He imports it from the city, but his supply is always gone by the time I get to the market."

Her brow wrinkled. Slate got the impression there was more to the story than that. Like perhaps the man was lying to her for some stupid mortal reason. Maybe he didn't like witches. Which was ridiculous. Every passing hour with Ruby revealed that she was a kind, irritatingly helpful person, and her being a witch should make them respect her more, not less. At least, that was what Slate found when he visited the mortal realm before Ruby came along.

Ruby unfolded the chocolate and paused. "Is it alright if I eat it here?"

Slate made it a rule not to eat in his nest unless he was

picking the bones clean. But he nodded, and Ruby broke off a piece and stuffed it in her mouth.

The chocolate did not look appealing with its hard and waxy appearance. But Ruby moaned in pleasure, the noise making Slate remember how she had looked stretched out around his fingers. His own hunger unfurled in his stomach, and for a moment, it even felt genuine. Like he did not just want to eat, he *needed* it. Like he might feel weak and useless if he didn't do it soon.

"I appreciate you going to all the effort," Ruby said, licking a shred of chocolate off her palm. It was already melting against her warm skin.

He tore her gaze away from the drop rolling down her wrist. "I must. Even with your dagger, you are still in danger. I will bring you food, and you can fetch water from the faucets. Stay out of the forest unless I am with you, or unless you absolutely have to wake me."

"I will," Ruby said and swallowed another piece of chocolate. "You've been... very good to me."

Slate snorted. But he could not find any trace of sarcasm in her tone, only gratefulness. And, he supposed, he *had* been good to her. Especially considering that he had been thinking about eating her when she appeared.

He still wanted to. But the want was melding with so many others it was getting hard to pick out his want to eat her from his want to—for instance—watch her eat chocolate. Or hold her down and push his tongue inside her. Or feel that dagger holster on her thigh again.

"I am bound to complete the warding ritual," he reminded her, ignoring all his writhing, unruly wants. "I cannot do that if you starve to death before we prepare you thoroughly."

Ruby flushed, as she so often did when he brought up what they had to do to complete the rite.

"I only mean to say thank you," she said. "Being a gracious host is yet another aspect of the dreaded Bygone they left out of the stories."

"Then that is one part they got correct. I have never hosted before."

She paused, her chewing slowing. "What about Paimon?"

Slate waved a dismissive claw. "Paimon left whenever he wished. I had no duty to host him. We spent most of our time outside this void, anyhow."

"Oh." Ruby picked distractedly at a patch of moss under her knees. "I thought you spent most of your time asleep."

"Before that," Slate said. "I did not spend all of my existence in this nest. Only the past few millennia."

Ruby's eyes grew round. Slate wondered what it was like to not be able to comprehend that length of time. Slate had been alive for so many human generations he probably seemed impossibly old to her.

Then again, he was impossibly old to most. Not much was older than him, except for the creatures who invented these voids in the first place. And as far as he knew, they were all dead.

"That sounds... peaceful," Ruby said slowly. "Lonely. But peaceful."

"*Lonely*." Slate snorted, his tail flicking. "I was picked for this void for a reason. I enjoy my solitude."

"You were *picked*?"

"Every elder Skullstalker was picked for their void. Not like the younglings, who stagger around any void they can find, wreaking destruction." He pointed at the chocolate melting in her hand. "You are dripping."

"What? Oh!" Ruby ran her tongue over her chocolate-streaked wrist. Her tongue was so small, and yet Slate could not tear his eyes away. His mind filled with memories: Ruby running her small tongue up his cock. Fitting it into his slit and licking away the salt. Rubbing it so tenderly over his knot—

"For someone who likes being alone so much," Ruby said quietly, fiddling with a feather jutting out next to her leg, "You don't seem too annoyed having me around."

Her heart was racing. He could smell the sweat on her skin. His mouth filled with saliva, which had been happening more since her arrival. At first, he assumed it was because of her soft, tantalizing meat. But the saliva usually occurred when he was thinking of devouring her in a very different way.

He loomed closer, watching her pupils swell. "Are you still sore?"

"I'm sensitive but not sore. I, um..." Ruby cringed. "I keep touching myself? Which isn't helping."

Slate didn't respond. He was lost for words, which was

such a rare occurrence he had no defense against it. The saliva pooling in his mouth was coming dangerously close to dripping down his chin. His eyelids drooped behind his mask as he imagined Ruby's lithe fingers slipping inside herself, stuffing her hole as full as she could manage.

Ruby's throat clicked. She shifted against his nest, getting her scent over it. She smelled *delectably* wet. He wanted to eat her whole.

"Do..." She hesitated, looking up to meet his half-lidded eyes. "Do you ever do that? Touch yourself?"

Slate suddenly wanted to rub her scent around his entire nest. To go to sleep in it. To strip her naked and watch her arch against the furs as he stretched her.

Ruby bit her lip. "Slate?"

He hadn't answered. He didn't want to tell her the truth: he very rarely touched himself.

His desires had sloughed away with age. His lust had gone the same way as his appetite. He had assumed they were gone for good. But with this little human cautiously stroking his belly, it was all slamming back into him faster than he could resist.

"Why should I?" he asked. "I have you."

With that, he surged forward and twisted her around until she was pressed chest-first into the nest.

Ruby moaned. She sounded shocked and, if he was reading her tone correctly, slightly appalled. Then he ground his hardening cock against her dress-clad ass, and everything melted out of the moan except for desperate hunger.

"I meant before..." she trailed off, gasping as he ran a

hand down her back and made the dress vanish. He watched the shadows roll away from her skin hungrily until she was completely naked in his nest.

He kept the dagger in its holster band around her thigh. They would not be attacked in his nest, but he liked how it looked against her skin.

"Before I got here," Ruby continued breathlessly as he pressed her naked breasts into the fur. "Did you go somewhere, find someone when you needed—*ohhhh*."

He felt her groan as he ran his tongue over her naked back. He reached around her torso, rolling her small breasts in his hands. He made sure to retract his claws this time, but only after pressing them into her skin and feeling the soft give.

"As I said," he rumbled in her ear. "I enjoy my solitude."

Ruby twisted her head, her dark eyes far too coherent for his liking. "But before, when you—when you needed release—"

Slate did not want to explain his previous lack of hunger when he was suddenly starving. He slid his tongue over her shoulder, fitting it into the grooves of her collarbone before wrapping it around her neck.

Moan, he thought desperately.

Ruby did. Slate felt it deliciously, her delicate neck vibrating against his tongue. He gave her a thankful squeeze, getting another moan in return, and slid his tongue down her spine, counting the notches.

"Spread your legs," he said.

Ruby did. Wetness gleamed on her thighs, and he

couldn't help himself from sliding his fingers over them and rubbing the slick into the fur underneath her.

Ruby's breath hitched. Did she recognize what he was doing? The idea made him feel strangely exposed. He wanted things so rarely. He didn't want her to see how badly he wanted her scent in his nest, surrounding him as he slept.

He withdrew his fingers from the wet fur of his nest and palmed her tight ass, ignoring how badly he wanted to sink his teeth into the flesh. Then he slid his tongue up her dagger-less thigh and into her wet, waiting hole.

Ruby jerked against his nest. A branch snapped underneath her, and Slate pictured fucking her until the woods were full of branches snapping, hips slapping, and Ruby's overwhelmed cries.

Not yet, he told herself. She still couldn't take his cockhead. They had a lot of work ahead of them.

He loosened her with his tongue through two whimpering orgasms. He meant to stop at one, but she was writhing against him so sweetly he forgot about it.

After she came the second time, sweet fluid gushing around his tongue and wetting his uncovered chin, he decided it was time.

He pulled his tongue out.

"Wait," she gasped. "I can—I can take it."

"I know," he soothed. "I'll give it to you, little witch."

With that, he slid two fingers into her and hooked them into her sweet spot. She howled, her muscles straining around him. It was a tight fit, but after several slick minutes of sliding in and out of her hole, he managed to fit a third finger inside her. At first, only the tip. Then it slid deeper and deeper until he could fuck her with all three.

Ruby groaned against his nest. Her mouth was open, the fur underneath damp with spit.

He pressed her head into it, grinding the dampness deeper. She groaned louder; the noise tinged with confusion. Maybe she *didn't* know he was scenting his nest, he thought, and felt a strange twist of relief and disappointment.

Slate didn't know how he had ever not been hungry for this. How he wasn't starving for it every second. Maybe he *should* have brought a mortal here whenever he needed it. But that conjured an image of some faceless stranger, and that wasn't right. It wouldn't be right unless it was Ruby, his strange little witch who bore down on his fingers even as she strained with effort.

"*Yes*," she groaned, muffled against the nest he was rubbing her face into. "Stretch me... train me for your cock. Make me useful, make me good. Oh, *gods*."

Slate spread his fingers. Ruby made a choked noise, hips working in a way that he now knew meant she was trying to get friction for her clit, which was pressed against the fur lining his nest.

Slate's cock throbbed painfully under his loincloth. He had been trying to will it down, telling himself to be patient. But she was stretching so beautifully around his fingers, and he couldn't resist.

He stood and flipped her over. Her chest heaved, breasts dripping with sweat from being trapped against the fur. There was a small pink mark on her leg where a feather had pressed into her.

I will have to layer the fur more deeply, Slate thought. *For her flimsy human skin.*

He knew he should be appalled at the idea of changing his nest for some mortal. But he only felt fiercely possessive as he bent down and licked the salt from her breasts. Then he swirled his tongue around her clit, listening to her sob with pleasure.

"I'm going to put my cock inside you now," he told her.

Ruby's eyes flew open. "But—"

Slate nuzzled her cheek, rumbling comfortingly. "Only what you can handle."

She still looked worried. He leaned over her and pressed a kiss to her shoulder. When he pulled back, there was an imprint of his bone mask on her skin.

He flicked his hand. His loincloth vanished in a cloud of shadows, and Ruby's mouth fell open as she watched his cock slap against his stomach.

"Only what you can handle," he repeated. "I promise."

Ruby nodded. She was shaking. She had started shaking before he even had his tongue inside her.

My responsive little mortal, he thought fondly. It took so little to get her wet and trembling. He wanted to ruin her.

He wiped his chin and rubbed the combination of his drool and her wetness onto his cockhead. Then he pressed it against her folds, spreading the slick.

"Slate," she begged.

He quite liked it when she said his name.

"Again," he commanded.

"Slate. Come on." She gave him a look that might have been frustrated if her eyes weren't so tearful and desperate.

He held her steady. Then he eased his cockhead into her hole. Just the very tip, rocking back the moment he felt resistance. Then he pressed forward with more force.

Ruby dug her teeth into her lip.

He slowed, eyeing the white skin around her teeth. "Is it too much?"

She shook her head. "It's just... a lot. Keep going."

He pushed forward again. Gentle pressure, rocking back and forth until his cockhead slid further in.

Ruby moaned, her back arching. Her dark hair was splayed out over his nest, her dark eyes gazing up at him in disbelief. She looked like a creature of shadows, like *his*.

Slate didn't realize he was close until he felt that telltale twitch in his knot.

"I'm going to," he started.

But it was too late. He came, spilling over her thighs and onto the fur lying underneath her. He had barely fit half his cockhead inside.

Ruby let out a shocked cry. She bucked against him, and his cockhead slid in a little deeper. His cock gave one last valiant twitch, and his knot thickened at his base.

Ruby sat up, her arms shaking with effort as she stared at the come dripping down her thighs.

"You can't get me pregnant, can you?"

"Skullstalkers cannot breed," he assured her. "Not as mortals do."

His cock softened inside her. He started to pull out, then paused.

"Ruby," he said.

Ruby sprawled back against the table, dazed and panting. "Slate?"

He pushed his soft cock deeper. His cockhead slipped in, and suddenly the slide was easier.

Ruby's legs spasmed. Her mouth opened with a silent yell, her back curving hard.

"Ruby," Slate prompted.

"*Yes*," she hissed.

Slate pushed in as far as he dared. There was still significant resistance, and he didn't want to hurt her. Not to mention, it was more difficult when he was soft. But slowly, carefully, he managed to feed several inches of his soft cock inside her.

Ruby wrapped her leg around his waist. "How much more is there?"

Slate looked down. "Most of it."

"Godsdamn Skullstalkers," Ruby said. But she was smiling, her face shining with sweat and triumph.

She was so beautiful. Slate wanted to eat her up. He leaned down, unsure what he was going to do until his lips pressed into hers.

She made a startled noise into his mouth. She tasted like chocolate and warmth, and something he couldn't identify that made him think of curling up somewhere safe and secluded.

He couldn't remember the last time he had kissed someone. Long before he had last fucked someone, he was sure.

Her cheek pressed into the edges of his skull mask. Her tongue grazed his fangs. It made him want to press closer, shove his soft cock deeper. Then he remembered how fragile she was and pulled back to examine her.

There was no blood in the air. He checked her mouth anyway, thumbing her jaw open to check inside.

"Thank you," Ruby panted.

He blinked. For checking he hadn't cut her?

"For the kiss," she said, surprisingly shy for someone he was still inside. "I didn't know if you wanted to."

"I shouldn't have," he tried. "My fangs—"

"We'll be careful," she said.

He touched her cheek. "My strange little witch."

"Strange?" she echoed. "For what? Wanting... this?"

She moved her hips. His soft cock would not fit any further, especially when it started to twitch and harden.

"I could eat you," he reminded her with a rough groan. "I considered it. You were not a lost soul, so I would have done it."

"I know." She leaned up like she was going to kiss him again, then hesitated. "Is it strange for you? Wanting a human?"

She sounded so timid. Like she was afraid of his answer. Like she was afraid he would tell her he wouldn't want her, which... yes, he was considering it. A lie would be easier than the truth. The truth was that he wanted her more than anything in millennia.

Not that he was going to admit that.

"It is strange wanting anything," he admitted. "I usually want very little."

Her shy expression dissolved into a relieved smile. "That's going to make our deal difficult. I have to give you whatever you want from me."

"Right," he said distractedly. "Yes."

He still hadn't considered what that might be. He wasn't about to start, with his cock hardening inside her.

Ruby's smile faltered. "Ouch."

Slate stilled. He had been rocking his hips and hadn't noticed.

"Do you want me to pull out?"

"Yes," she said hurriedly.

He reluctantly pulled out of her tight warmth. His half-hard cock bounced in the cool forest air, and he concentrated on willing it to go down. But Ruby was still naked and drenched in his nest, which proved to be antithetical to his objective.

He stood, turning away. "I trust you do not remember the way back to the castle. I will lead you."

Ruby didn't respond. He turned back to see Ruby pushing herself up on her knees, leaning out of the nest toward his naked groin.

Slate thought about refusing her. But her lips were red and puffy from kissing, and he found he couldn't look away as she leaned in.

"This does not prepare you," he reminded her as she

wrapped her hands around his hardening cock. "It is useless."

"It doesn't feel useless." She shot him a shy smile. "You made me come over and over. Let me return the favor."

Then she pressed her lips to his cock, and all reason slid happily from Slate's head.

Eleven

Slate looked different when he was asleep.

Soft. Oddly tender. Also, he curled up like a cat, which made Ruby think of the word *adorable*—as if it could ever be applied to a Skull-stalker.

He would be decidedly *less* adorable once he woke up. Ruby was deciding whether a trek back through the forest was worth it after spending all this time finding her way here from the castle. But if she got attacked by demons, she'd never hear the end of it. If she even survived long enough for him to berate her.

She sighed. Then she reached out and touched him cautiously on the shoulder.

"Slate?"

Nothing. Slate didn't even flinch.

She pushed harder on his shoulder. Slate's tail flicked out and swatted her arm away with such force that she stumbled back.

"Ow," she muttered. She raised her voice reluctantly. "Slate!"

Slate rumbled low in his chest. One eyelid pried open, his black eye fixing on her.

For a moment he said nothing. He just lay there and stared, his curled body cushioned by feathers and furs, which she could have sworn had gotten thicker since she was here last.

Then he growled, pushing himself up on his elbows. "I told you not to come into the forest unless I was present."

"Or unless I needed you," she corrected.

Slate's growl turned into an annoyed grumble. "I barely had time to nap."

"It's been two days," Ruby replied awkwardly.

Slate frowned sleepily. "Do you need food?"

"No," Ruby replied, thinking of the dried meat, fruit, and oats she had piled up in the drawers beside her bed. "The last batch could last me weeks if I needed."

"Then what?"

Ruby paused. She had said it several times now. But it was still hard to say, especially when he said it so much better.

She waited until his eyes went half-lidded, his swishing tail stilling against the nest.

"You're ready again?" he asked, his voice low and silky.

Ruby shifted on the spot, feeling the flat of the shadow dagger press against her thigh. She was still tender inside from last time. But she could take it.

She nodded.

Slate surged up and grabbed her waist.

Ruby's breath thudded out of her as he threw her into his nest. Sometimes they did this in her bed, but more often nowadays they did it in his nest. She was starting to prefer it, and she suspected he did too. He was always rubbing her fluids into the furs like he wanted evidence of her there later. Or maybe that was pure instinct and didn't mean anything at all.

Slate leaned over her, his loincloth already thrown to the forest floor.

"Open your legs," he purred.

Ruby shivered and did.

The next day, Ruby explored the kitchen.

She walked carefully. The day after taking his cock was always when she was the most sensitive. Even her thighs ached from her brief attempt at riding him.

Ruby stared up at the towering stone counter. It was almost up to her neck; she could hardly cut up her skinned rabbit on it.

She sighed and turned toward the oven. Through several mistakes that led to her smoking out the room, she finally discovered that it did not work like the clay oven in her cottage. Instead, there were tiny dials on top that, when pressed, made an enchantment on the side of the oven glow blue. Then the oven would warm up, getting hotter the more she turned the dial.

No wood needed. No coal, not even oil. Just a dial

and a glowing enchantment that Slate didn't seem to know anything about.

"I never come in here," Slate explained when she asked about it. "I have no use for cooked meat."

Ruby slung the rabbit over her shoulder and dragged over a chair that she had found in a nearby room. It was metal, which had to be why it hadn't rotted yet. But it was covered in rust, and she grimaced as she climbed onto it. It felt like it would cave at any second.

Slate's rough voice spoke up from the door. "A fire seems easier."

Ruby looked over from her precarious position in front of the oven. She could reach the dials from here—barely. The chair only pushed her up so far.

"A fire *would* be easier," she replied. "But I'm not in the mood to twirl a spit. If I can make this oven work, I can walk away until it's done."

She strained to reach the main dial.

Slate stepped forward. "I can do it."

"I got it," she said, winded. Her stomach pressed into the oven.

She flicked the dial on with a triumphant noise. The enchantment on the side flickered to life, blaring blue light.

Ruby jumped back to the floor and rearranged the skinned rabbit hanging over her shoulder. "There! Now all I need to do is cut this up, and I have a few days of meals."

Slate eyed the tall countertops that Ruby would

strain to reach even with the chair. "And how do you plan to do that?"

"Well," Ruby said, trying to keep her smile. "I was just going to use the knife you made me and..."

Slate took the rabbit from her shoulder and dumped it onto the counter. Then he started dragging his claw over it.

Ruby watched him, surprised. He was cutting it into sections, the way she would do it. Had he been watching mortals again, figuring out how to cook?

She leaned her chin on the countertop, straining to even do that.

"What lived here?" she asked in a rush. "Before you."

Slate grunted, pushing his claw between the rabbit's shoulders. "Nothing that exists today."

Ruby paused. He said it in the same tone that he had answered her questions about the enchantment that powered the oven: like he didn't know the full story and didn't want her to guess.

Ruby looked around the giant kitchen at the rusted implements she didn't recognize and the strange contraptions among the counters. Whatever society had built this, Ruby had heard nothing about it. She had been taught that Skullstalkers came to life along with every other spirit, and mortals came not long after. There was nothing before Skullstalkers—or at least, that was what Ruby had been told.

"Why do I know nothing of them?" Ruby asked.

"Mortals know little of the voids."

"Yes, but..." Ruby bit her lip. "There would be evidence of them in the mortal realm, wouldn't there?"

"There is. You simply don't recognize it." Slate gathered the rabbit chunks in his claws and held them out. "Here you go."

"Oh! Thank... you." Not knowing what else to do, Ruby let him pile them in her arms.

Slate turned to leave.

"Thank you," Ruby repeated as he exited. Then she sighed, nose wrinkling in disgust at the rabbit meat dampening her dress. She would have to get him to re-materialize it after she was finished in here. She wished she knew how to do it herself—as long as he still had control over it, too. A big draw of this dress was how he could wave it away with a flick of his wrist.

She dragged out a tray and set it on the floor, ignoring the rust but also the disappointment in her stomach.

Just because you're staying in his void doesn't mean he wants to stay and chat, she reminded herself. *He said it himself: he values his solitude.*

But she couldn't help the sadness as she leaped to drag the oven door open again, holding up a hand to shield herself from the burst of hot air that clouded out. She had been hoping that he would ask if she was ready for another training session, as he often did when he came into the castle. The answer would have been no, but she liked to be asked. It made her stomach swoop in excitement every time, thinking of when she could finally say yes again.

If only he would stay after, Ruby thought as she heaved the oven door shut on the tray of rabbit meat. She was growing tired of waking up alone in her castle bed every time she fell asleep in his arms.

Two days and a prolonged practice session later, Ruby limped back into the kitchen and gasped.

Stairs. Metal stairs welded onto every counter and even the oven door, climbing so high Ruby could reach them without strain.

There was something piled on top of the nearest counter. Ruby bounded up the new stairs and shrieked in delight.

Knives. Dishtowels. Pots that weren't made for giants and covered in rust. Bowls. Salt! And not just any salt, *her* salt, with the familiar containers that rested on her windowsill. It looked like Slate had emptied out her entire kitchen back home, plus a few miscellaneous items from nearby, like a stray peg. He didn't know what belonged in a kitchen, after all.

She turned to find him looming in the kitchen doorway, shadows flickering strangely around his skull.

Ruby gestured at the pile on the counter. "What are *these*?"

"I assumed you would recognize them."

Ruby giggled. "That's not what I meant! You really did this for me?"

Slate's tail swished. He took a breath, and it was several seconds before he spoke.

"I was bored," he replied.

Ruby's words stuck in her throat. She wanted to tell him how grateful she was that he would do this for her when she was with him for such a short time. She wanted to tell him how much she missed her little cottage, how happy it made her to feel all her chipped knives with warped handles she'd used every day of her adult life. To tell him that no one had done anything so kind for her since the last witch of Sweetsguard died.

"Thank you," she whispered. "It means... *thank you*."

Slate nodded. He wasn't looking at her, and his tail was swishing even faster now.

"Do not mention it," he said gruffly. Then he coughed a sharp, guttural bark that used to make Ruby jump.

"How are you feeling?"

Ruby shifted against the stairs he'd built for her. She felt very tender. But she could take his tongue, at the very least. And she wanted to show him how truly grateful she was.

"Ready," she said.

His eyes locked on hers. Ruby's spine tingled, warmth pooling between her sore legs as he loomed closer.

"Good," he rumbled. "As am I."

TWELVE

Ruby didn't know how long she had been in this void.

It was still evening. The same one, if she wasn't mistaken. But she had lost track of how many times she slept.

She was also losing track of how many times he had been inside her.

They were still nowhere near his knot. She had only managed to fit half his cock, and only because of several sessions where he stayed inside... after.

He could get deeper the second time. Sometimes he got deeper on the third. By the fourth, Ruby was usually too sore to take any more.

Except for his tongue. They quickly figured out that they both thoroughly enjoyed it when he licked his spend out of her afterward.

But before that, there were the in-between times. When he was soft inside her, waiting to get hard again.

Those were some of Ruby's favorite times, lying with him and asking him about his void.

"We do not all have our own voids," he told her as they lay in his nest together after their first round. "Only the eldest."

"Like you," Ruby said drowsily. It was a strange sensation; she was stretched so thoroughly, her hole pulsing around him. But she was also exhausted from their extended session, her eyelids fluttering even as she ached for more.

"Like me," Slate said quietly. He ran a hand down her back. He had been touching her more after their first time in his nest. A hand on her back to guide her somewhere, or stroking her hair behind her ears.

It was lovely. It made Ruby feel like he wanted her even when she wasn't training to take his cock.

She toyed with a feather poking out of the nest by her hip. "What are the younger Skullstalkers like?"

"I have not met many," Slate admitted. "But the younglings I *have* met are foolhardy. Vicious, if not outright feral. Many of them stalk the mortal realm for easy prey. They delight in the hunt."

That sounded more like the Skullstalkers Ruby had learned about as a child. She shivered, imagining appearing in Slate's void to find a creature just as monstrous as she had expected.

Slate's stomach gurgled under her cheek.

Ruby laughed, shocked. "Is all this talk of hunting making you hungry?"

Slate didn't reply. When she lifted her head, he was

staring up at the trees. The shadows around his mask flickered anxiously.

Ruby sat up, careful not to dislodge his slowly hardening cock inside her. "Slate?"

"I do not hunger often," Slate said finally. "Not truly."

"Is that a problem?" Ruby asked faintly, her mind racing with possibilities. "Are you... afraid of losing control?"

Slate made a noise deep in his throat, half-chirp, half snort. A surprised laugh, she realized.

"You have nothing to fear from me," he assured her. "The urge is simply... disconcerting. I am not used to it."

He sat up, adjusting her against his lap. Ruby let him move her and thought back to him admitting that he didn't *want* many things, so wanting her was new for him. If a basic urge like hunger felt strange, lust must really be odd for him.

Not to mention any other wants. Ruby wasn't assuming anything, but he seemed to enjoy their time together. Even if most of it involved stretching her around his cock.

"Do you..." Ruby trailed off in a moan as he gripped her thighs, holding her up above the generous amount of half-hard cock she still couldn't fit. "Slate. You eat humans, right?"

"I did," Slate said and paused. "I do."

He was thickening inside her. Ruby groaned, digging her fingers into his arms. She had been gentle at first before remembering that he was a literal monster and could easily take some mortal squeezing him.

She clenched around him, feeling him twitch in response.

"Would you really have eaten me?" she asked breathily. "If I didn't bind you?"

"Yes." His hands tightened under her thighs, pulling her another aching inch onto his hardening cock. "I still long for it. I would hold myself back, even with the binding, but I am—"

He cut off with a growl, nuzzling into her throat. "I am glad you bound me. At times, it is difficult not to devour you whole."

He lifted her completely, suspending her in the air above the nest. She let her head fall against his smooth, pale chest, glad for the cool skin against her overheated forehead.

Ruby moaned. He had just told her he struggled not to *eat* her; it should have terrified her. Instead, she was strangely touched. She truly believed him when he said he would continue holding himself back without the binding. He would do that for her.

"I'm glad too," she gasped as he started to move inside her. "I... I would have never—*oh*."

The words flew out of her head as he fucked softly into her, his cock fully hard and stretching her to her limit. Wet sounds filled the forest. Come dripped down his cock, slicking the way.

"You are taking more of me," Slate said, hips working

gently. "Soon you will be able to fit all of me. And then my knot."

Ruby whined and looked down at where their bodies joined. There was still so much of him to take. His knot sat thick and hard at his base, making her mouth water every time.

"I want it," she whispered. "Slate, I want it so much. I wish I could take it now. Wish I could've taken it that first day when you bent me over that ward. Wish—"

He pulled out to the tip of his cockhead and then pushed inside again. One long, deliciously thick slide that stopped when he was only halfway in, and Ruby cut off in a desperate moan.

It was a half-truth. She *did* wish she had been able to take him that first day. But she was also deeply glad she couldn't. If she had, she would never have gotten this: slow, careful rocking as he forced himself deeper. She would have never learned what it felt like to be filled and fucked and filled again, would have never known what it felt like to have a shadow dress vanish under his touch. Never known what his nest felt like, delicious furs rubbing against her open mouth. Never known what he looked like when he wanted to shove deeper but was forcing himself not to.

She would have never kissed him.

Slate grunted, holding her still while he fucked her. "I am close."

"Do it," she begged.

He crushed her to his chest and came. She felt him pulse inside her, slicking her stuffed channel. Wave after wave until it dripped out over his cock, then down his balls and onto the nest. The long, hot spurt of it was nearly enough to make her follow him over.

But all too soon, it was done. He panted hard, his tongue lolling out to lick an absentminded stripe up her cheek. He often did that when she was dripping sweat, but now it made her remember how hungry he was. She shivered around his softening cock, imagining him chasing her through the dark forest and pinning her down, those big fangs closing over her neck.

At times, it is difficult not to devour you whole, he had said.

Some part of her wanted him to.

"I've made a mess of you," Slate rumbled against her hair. "Let me clean that up."

Ruby groaned as he slipped out of her. A torrent of come gushed out with it, soaking the furs below.

He pushed her onto her back. Ruby went gladly, reveling in the softness. The furs *were* thicker than their first time here, she was sure of it now. It made her stomach squirm pleasantly, thinking he could have done it for her comfort. Then again, maybe it was just time to add more furs.

He held her legs apart and slid his long tongue up her thighs, collecting the pearly trails that had dripped over her legs.

"Hungry beast," she breathed.

He growled against her thigh. His fangs pressed into her skin, and for a heart-stopping moment, Ruby wasn't sure what he was going to do.

Then his fangs retreated, and his tongue returned. It slid straight into her dripping hole, and any heated worries about getting eaten were replaced with the pure rapture of getting *eaten*, his long, thick tongue licking his spend out of her.

Ruby squirmed. Not for the first time, she wished he would let her sleep here. No matter where they "practiced," she would wake up alone in her castle bed. Just once, she wanted to wake up to his soft rumbling, the feeling of fur on her face and cool arms wrapped around her.

This will have to be enough, she told herself. Then his tongue curled inside her, and Ruby thought of nothing but pleasure.

Several hours later—or thereabouts, it was hard to tell when the evening light remained unchanged—Ruby sat at the castle entrance, watching the tree line.

The dog spirit rested its head in her lap, breathing deeply. She didn't think spirits could sleep, but this one made a damn good impression of it.

Every once in a while, it would lift its head and look at her curiously.

"Not yet," she told it.

The dog dropped its head back into her lap.

Ruby stroked the dog, her eyes returning to the trees.

Slate said he would be back soon. At least, she thought he said that. She had been falling asleep when he said it, rocked in his giant arms as he carried her back to the palace.

She adjusted her old dress over her knees. It had been draped over a chair when she woke up, thanks to a particularly embarrassing morning where she woke up after a night of preparing only to realize he wasn't around to magic her shadow dress back on. She had wandered naked around the castle for hours until she finally found the anointing room where he stroked blue liquid onto her naked body. Her dress and cloak had been just where she left them.

It had been a good opportunity to map out the castle. She just wished she didn't have to be naked and shivering for it.

He had been apologetic when he finally showed up. It hadn't occurred to him that she couldn't magic her own clothes on. Ruby had tried to be mad at him, but this was a creature who barely needed to eat or drink and could transport her miles away with a touch. Of course, he would forget simple things like wearing clothes.

A large shape loped out of the trees.

Ruby stood. She usually spent her alone time exploring the void, cooking in the giant kitchen, or playing with the dog spirit, but she wanted to see what happened after he came back from a hunt. She told herself it was so she would be reminded he was a Skull-stalker, not something she could ever have a future with. But if she was honest, she wanted to see the feral, inhuman creature inside him for other reasons. Reasons that made her tender hole throb with need.

Another rustle in the trees.

The dog spirit's head snapped up. His tail thumped happily.

"I know," she told him.

Slate appeared out of the trees. He was smeared with blood, long tongue licking his skull mask clean as he lumbered out of the trees.

Then he froze. He had spotted Ruby.

Ruby lifted her hand in a silent wave.

Slate waved a hesitant hand back. He wasn't wearing his loincloth. His skin was bone-pale, which only looked paler in contrast to the blood coating his body. His skull mask was dripping with it, gore hanging off his bare chin.

The dog spirit barked and took off, tail high.

Ruby followed him. Slate seemed reluctant to move, petting the dog distractedly until Ruby arrived in front of him.

"How was the hunt?" Ruby asked.

Slate blinked. There was a shred of flesh on his eyelashes.

"Good," he said cautiously.

"What did you eat?" Ruby asked, bracing herself. She was determined not to balk if he told her it was a human. Unless he hunted near Sweetsguard. Then she would have to ask.

"A demon."

Ruby frowned, remembering the thin, ashy limbs of the demons she'd seen. "A shade?"

"No, a kobald. It was in another void." Slate wiped a

hand over his bloody jaw, only succeeding in smearing the mess instead of cleaning it.

Ruby nodded, keeping her face blank. Then she asked a question that surprised both of them. "Can I see it next time?"

Slate didn't move. The dog spirit barked, jumping to lick his dripping hand.

"You cannot eat," he told the spirit. He turned back to Ruby and said, "I was last hungry several years ago. You will not be around next time."

"Oh." Ruby forced a smile, hiding her disappointment and trying to figure out why she was so disappointed in the first place. Why did she *want* to watch the monster she was sleeping with rip a demon apart with his teeth?

"That's fine," she said.

Slate grunted. Even though she couldn't see his expression under his mask, his averted eyes were enough.

"Is something wrong?" she asked carefully.

Slate made another noise. A wet gurgle, like there was something meaty stuck in his throat.

"I thought it would be decades until I hunted again," he said. "My hunger has gotten weaker with age. Until you came along. The fact that I would eat after mere years is... disconcerting."

Ruby laughed. No wonder he had been baffled that she needed to eat multiple times a day.

"A kobald would have been more than enough, last time," Slate continued slowly. "Now I am... I am still not full."

"Is that so bad?" Ruby asked. "There will be other kobalds."

"I am not worried about running out of things to hunt. I am worried about..." Slate growled, and the prey-animal instinct filled Ruby with adrenaline. Getting her ready to run. To be *chased*.

"Changing," Slate admitted.

Ruby pushed down her instincts telling her to get out of there as fast as she could. It was shockingly easy, especially with Slate looking so morose.

"Changing," Ruby repeated. "In a good way or a bad way?"

"I am not certain." Slate petted the dog spirit, who had started nudging his leg with its head. Ruby was glad nothing stuck to the dog's fur, otherwise it would be streaked with blood.

Ruby twisted her old dress nervously, her heart pounding in her chest.

He wasn't the only one changing. This void was doing something to her. Making her magic more powerful. But she was now the kind of woman who knew what a Skullstalker felt like inside her—cock, fingers, tongue. She knew how to navigate his castle and some of his forest. She knew secrets the mortal realm had kept from her.

How could she go back to her normal life after this? Would she spend her days living alone on the edge of that tiny town, reminiscing on the brief time she spent training to take a Skullstalker's cock for a ritual?

She touched her old dress. It felt so thick and

scratchy on her now. Would he let her keep the shadow dress, or would it dissolve the second she stepped back into her realm?

"I should get cleaned up," Slate said, looking down at his bare, bloody body.

Ruby pulled herself out of her spiraling thoughts. She watched him take a step toward the castle, an idea forming in her whirling head.

She touched his arm. "I could give you a bath."

Slate cocked his head. "You do not have to."

"I want to." She rubbed his arm, only remembering too late what he was covered in. Her fingers were coated in blood now, a thread of flesh sticking to her palm. She waited for the disgust to set in.

But it didn't come. She was a witch, after all. She was used to a little blood.

Slate inclined his head. "If you wish it."

They turned toward the castle. His gaze lingered on her dress, as it often did when he saw her wearing her old clothes.

"You're stained," he pointed out.

Ruby frowned and looked down. There was a spot of blood on her hem from where she had stood far too close. She looked up at him, waiting for him to draw out the blood like he had done the last time she stained her dress.

"It is not my blood," Slate said, frustrated. "I cannot vanish it."

"Oh." Ruby held it up, wondering about the

perfumed soap she found in his bathroom and whether it would get out bloodstains. Then she paused.

"Then I'll have to wear something else," she said.

He stood back, expectant.

Ruby looked around. The forest was empty except for them and the dog spirit, who was snuffling at some bushes in the distance.

She gathered her dress and pulled it over her head. The cool air on her bare skin made her nipples harden, goosebumps spreading over parts of her that had never felt a breeze.

Slate curled a finger. Shadows climbed over Ruby's skin, draping her in black. A holster band hugged her thigh, and Ruby shifted on the spot to feel the dagger press into the tender skin.

"Thank you," she whispered.

Slate stepped closer, his gaze fixed on her. His chin gleamed with blood. His mouth was wet with it.

Ruby wanted to kiss him anyway.

She was leaning up when a far-off yelp echoed through the trees.

She jumped. "What was that?"

Slate shushed her. His head was tilted, listening intently.

Another yelp rang through the trees. Sounds of a scuffle quickly cut off.

Then horrible silence.

Thirteen

Slate knotted his loincloth over his sticky skin as they ran, shadows swishing around his thighs.

"Is he okay?" Ruby called from where she was lagging behind him. "Can you sense him?"

Slate couldn't. There was a spell blocking him from sensing the spirit. But he *could* sense the demons that took him: shades, their scent thick and acrid in his nostrils.

Ruby panted behind him, holding her shadow skirt as she ran. She was wincing, and it took Slate a moment to realize that he hadn't given her shoes when he conjured her dress.

He turned and scooped her up. She slammed against his bare chest, her breath whooshing out of her.

Slate loosened his grip. It was so easy to forget how fragile she was, especially when she was racing toward danger with him.

"We're getting close," he assured her. "I have their trail. They're right—"

He stumbled to an abrupt stop.

A glowing rip in reality waited in front of them. It was not a portal, something carefully opened by a witch or sorcerer. But a crude, ugly tear between realms by some careless nobodies with no regard for inter-realm integrity.

Slate growled and reached out, stabilizing the tear with a wave of his hand.

"Is that a portal?" Ruby asked, nose scrunching at the careless composition. "Where does it lead?"

"The mortal realm," Slate replied. He ran a bloody finger along the newly repaired edges, stretching it until it was wide enough to step through. "Ready?"

"To go home?" Ruby looked at the glowing portal and let out a strange, thin laugh. "As long as you bring me back after."

The words made something twist in Slate's chest. He had to stop himself from crushing her closer and vowing something he had no right to say.

"Be ready," he warned.

Then he stepped through the portal.

They touched down on dry, cracked cobblestones.

Slate set Ruby on the ground and looked around. They were in the middle of Sweetsguard's empty town square, the first dawn light peeking out over the squat buildings.

The portal tear sealed behind him. Slate glanced over to see Ruby holding her black dagger, blood beading on her finger from closing the tear.

Slate had the bizarre urge to take her wounded finger and kiss it. He settled for giving her a brisk nod.

She nodded back. But halfway through the motion, her eyes caught on something over his shoulder, and she gasped.

Slate turned.

Paimon's stone ward sat behind him, lodged in the dirt. It was identical to the one in his own realm, complete with the fading blue rune. Except where the Paimon ward in his domain was clean, save for a few stray leaves, this ward had been strewn with filth.

Ruby ran to it, wiping at the mud and oil with her hands. She checked the rune worriedly, her shoulders sagging with relief when she confirmed it was active.

"Still working," she said with a sigh. She picked sadly at a particularly deep crack in the stone and gave Slate a rueful smile. "I suppose we'd know if it stopped. Demons would pour over the town before we could say—"

A horrified scream cut her off.

Slate turned.

The pie woman—*Glenda*, he reminded himself— was standing frozen at the edge of the town square, a bundle of clothes at her feet where she had dropped them. Her face was set in such dramatic terror that Slate wanted to chuckle.

Ruby raised her hand. "Hello, Glenda."

Glenda screamed again, her face ruddy. She was shaking, her eyes flicking between the two of them like she didn't know what to be more scared of—Slate, with his shadows leaking behind his skull mask and his chin dripping with gore, larger than any mortal she'd ever seen, or Ruby, dressed in matching shadows and a dagger made of night held in her hand.

"It's not what you think," Ruby tried.

This only made Glenda screech louder. She stumbled back, horrified tears pooling in her eyes.

"It's the B-Bygone," she cried. "The Bygone has come to break the ward and take us as his eternally damned servants! Flee for your lives!"

"We're not breaking the ward," Ruby argued.

Slate leaned down. "It's not worth talking to this mortal. We need to go."

"But the dog spirit," Ruby started.

Slate pointed into the woods in the distance. "They went in there. I can smell them. Are you coming with me or would you like to get reacquainted with your townsfolk?"

Ruby looked at Glenda, who was trying to scrape the fallen clothes back into her arms while she fled. She was still screaming, her face blotchy with panicked tears.

"I think I'll go with you," Ruby said.

Slate stared around the strange, shadowless trees.

"She'll never shut up about that," Ruby said, sliding her dagger back into her thigh holster. "What was she saying? *Damned servant?* And I'm wearing your shadows, *and* you're *covered* in blood!"

Slate lashes his tail, irritated. He thought she *liked* wearing his shadows. And she hadn't seemed very bothered by him being covered in blood before, even after he had worried about it.

"She should watch her tongue," he snarled.

It came out even more savagely than he intended. Savage enough that Ruby stopped, her brows rising.

"Or what?" she asked. "Will the dreaded Bygone take her as a damned servant?"

"I have no use for servants," Slate snapped. "I…"

He tried to stop his tail, which was lashing so hard it clouded up the plain, boring leaves. Her discomfort unsettled him in ways he didn't fully understand. There was so much he didn't understand about himself since she had shown up. For millennia, he had a quiet, sensible existence. Then she appeared and suddenly he was lusting and hunting and *wanting*. The only thing that made any of it worth it was the ridiculous rapture she afforded him.

And soon, it would be gone. They would renew the ward, and she would leave. Existence would return to normal. No more rapture, no more uncertainty.

Unless…

Slate blinked, the idea setting up dark roots.

Unless he *made* her stay. They were bound. After he renewed the ward, she had to do something for him. It could be anything.

Ruby moved closer. "Slate?"

Slate pulled himself out of his swirling thoughts. His tail wasn't lashing anymore. Instead, it was wrapped around her wrist, pulling her close. She was frowning, the stark light of the mortal realm making her dark dress look pitifully pale.

I thought you liked being mine, he thought.

He forcibly loosened his tail from her wrist and stepped back. "She should still watch her tongue. I should eat *her* next for the things she has said about you."

Ruby's frown deepened. "What things? Since when do you know the things my neighbor says about me?"

Slate hesitated. He had never specified where he found her chocolate, nor any of the food he had been bringing her. Most of it was from the townsfolk of Sweetsguard, who were starting to complain about a thief.

"Your town disrespects you," he replied. "You should not tolerate it."

Ruby shook her head with a dry laugh. "Even before my magic showed, I was different. Too quiet, too shy. Then I discovered my magic and started my witch training, and they said I was putting on airs. I just wish..."

She sighed bitterly. "I wish I didn't want them to like me so much. I still want it, even after everything. I used to pray to Paimon for it."

It sounded like a ridiculous thing to pray for. Then again, Slate had never wished for anyone to like him. Solitude had been enough for him. It would be enough again after she left.

"I would've given anything," she said quietly. Then she straightened, her chin lifting into the defiance he was growing stupidly fond of. "Anyway, however much they dislike me now, I expect it will only get *worse* now that they've seen that. They might force me out of town."

Slate growled. "Let them try."

"And what, you'll eat them? That will only get me feared throughout the mortal realm. The Bygone's servant, indeed." She rubbed her eyes, which were dangerously close to tears, and then gave him a tight smile.

"Come on," she said. "You said you smelled the trail here?"

She started to turn away. Slate grabbed her arm, forcing her back. He was hot with fury, his shadows lashing the stale air around him.

"You are kind and selfless," he growled. "You bound yourself to me even when you thought it meant your death. They should *worship* you for it."

Ruby gaped. She was blushing, the red flush running down her neck, and Slate thought about wrapping his tongue around it.

"I—" Ruby started. She ran a hand through her long hair, grimacing when she noticed the mud remaining from cleaning the ward. "Dammit. Why would demons steal a dog spirit? Is that something they do?"

"Not typically," Slate said. "They cannot eat him. It must be to spite me."

He cursed himself silently. First, he was not aware of souls withering in his realm until they turned into shades, and now he was letting innocent dog spirits get stolen.

"To spite you," Ruby repeated. "Why?"

He raised his head and sniffed. Bark, insects, dirt that was somehow less appealing than the dirt in his realm. And underneath it, the acrid stench of shade demons.

"I will follow their trail," he said. "You stay here."

Ruby spluttered indignantly and shoved in front of him. "What for? I might not be able to snatch demons out of midair, but I *am* a witch. *And* I'm armed. *And*—"

Slate bent down, trying to use his height to menace her for the first time in days. Or possibly weeks. Time was malleable in his void.

"And what?" he demanded.

He expected her to wilt. To apologize, however grudgingly.

Instead, she looked him straight in the eye, his darkness reflecting onto her.

"And I'm with you," she reminded him. "You won't let me get hurt."

A shocked growl rumbled through his chest. She had been practically cowering from him in those early days. Now she didn't even flinch. Her cheeks were bright, her face set in stunned disbelief like even she was amazed by her own nerve.

Slate stared at her, his growl dying. She was less than half his height. Bones that snapped like toothpicks. Skin that parted like paper. And she was glaring at him like she would fight him right here with only her weak mortal magic and the knife he conjured for her.

Slate wanted to kiss her so badly it ached.

"Fine," He snapped. "But I don't want any dawdling."

With that, he swept her into his arms and started after the trail.

FOURTEEN

Ruby watched the trees rush past and realized something shocking: she missed the shadows.

She had been so terrified of them the first time she appeared in Slate's void. But now, nestled against Slate's cool chest as he sprinted through the forest, she found she kept searching for the shadows dripping off the branches.

There were none. Which was... good. Wasn't it? Before Ruby stepped into his void, she would have said it meant safety. Now she ached for them. She ached for Slate's whole realm: the twisty, crumbling castle, the dark forest, and his deceptively soft nest.

It would be an adjustment, to come back. For all she wished the town would warm to her, she had long since accepted it wouldn't happen. But Slate...

His arm curled protectively over her head as they passed a series of low branches.

Ruby smiled against his chest. *Slate* was warming to

her. His growls had gotten so much less frequent, and he touched her so softly, even when he was holding her face down on her bed. Even when he was visibly holding himself back from devouring her.

Not that he would want her there all the time. He liked his solitude, as he said. And he seemed genuinely disturbed by her short lifespan. Even if he did want her to stay, she doubted he would allow it for the very same reasons why she had never adopted a pet rat—their lives were too damn short.

"We are coming up to them," Slate warned. "Their stench is getting closer."

Ruby nodded, reaching down to touch the dagger hidden under her dress. Back to the issue at hand: the demons they were running toward. She hoped the dog spirit was okay. If he wasn't, she would join Slate in ripping these demons apart. Her magic was weaker in the mortal realm—she could already feel it fade inside her— but she would burn all the magic she had to make them pay.

She looked up at Slate. "If they hurt that dog, I'm going to fry their skin from their bones."

Slate's eyes widened behind his mask. He let out a low, amused rumble.

"Not if I beat you to it," he promised.

If Ruby wasn't so worried, she would have smiled. It wasn't in her nature to harm; she was a helpful witch. But for these demons, she would allow it.

A sharp yip made them both jerk. Ruby struggled against his grip, fighting to get to the ground.

"Stay close," he growled as he lowered her to the forest floor.

She took the dagger out of her thigh holster and nodded. She stared around the trees, wishing that she had been more serious about hunting. Knowing how to make traps for birds and rabbits didn't feel worth much with demons waiting to jump on her.

Slate slowed. Ruby looked up to see him stumble to a stop at the mouth of an old, ruined cottage. The straw and wood had rotted away, leaving only a stone archway, a gate, and the impression of a foundation.

Slate grunted.

"What is it?" Ruby asked. Something was itching at the back of her head, her fingers tingling like they did after she cast a spell. She shook her fingers out, suddenly sweating around her dagger. They were itching to touch the archway, she realized.

She stepped up beside him and reached up to touch the stones scored with age and moss.

Slate started, "This was once—"

Another loud yip rang through the forest. Then an alarmed screech, followed by pattering paws.

The dog spirit burst through the trees, its transparent tongue lolling. It sprinted through the remains of the cottage, and a half-dozen angry yowls went up.

Shade demons appeared in the trees behind him, their ashy skin crackling with rage.

"*The dog ruined it*," one of them rasped. "*Kill the spirit!*"

"*We can still do it,*" the next one argued, his voice so full of spikes Ruby shuddered. "*Set it off! Set it off!*"

Before Ruby could ask what *it* was, a giant net fell through the trees. It slammed into the remains of the cottage, taking the stone archway out with it.

Slate's strong arm wrapped around Ruby, shoving her back just before the net came down over her head. But his own arm got caught, and he slammed into the ground with a roar.

Ruby tumbled to the ground, already confused even as the breath whooshed out of her. It was just a net. What could make Slate roar like that?

The dog spirit ran to her side, barking. It nosed at her side as Ruby stumbled up and gasped.

The net wasn't made of ropes, like she had assumed. It was knotted together with some strange black vine pricked with white flowers, pinning Slate's arm to the ground with an unnatural force. His skin blistered under its touch, deep burns scoring into the skin.

The stench of burned flesh filled the air. The dog spirit barked wildly, its teeth bared.

The demons shrieked with disbelief and laughter. Except for the one who had ordered the net to fall.

"*Only his arm,*" the shade demon yelled. "*He'll get through that in a second! Attack!*"

Several of them started to fly toward him. Ruby ran ahead, throwing herself over Slate's arm and slicing at the ropes.

Slate snarled. He was already ripping with her, his

fingers blistering and his claws cracking as he tore the net from his skin.

The dog spirit barked louder. Ruby could barely hear it over the demons shrieking, which got closer and closer until—

The net snapped. Slate roared so loud her ears rang and leaped over her, covering her with his body.

He shoved her into his chest. For a moment, Ruby saw nothing but pale skin and listened as he twisted and clawed at the demons descending.

Then his arm shifted, and Ruby could see it all.

There were three demons left. A fourth was crumbling against a tree, crisping the leaves as it burned to dust. A fifth was in Slate's crushing grip, scrabbling at Slate's burned hand. The dog spirit was barking madly, trying to bite a demon and only succeeding in bumping it backward.

One of the remaining demons screeched and dove at Slate's back.

Ruby slammed him with a fireball. It was so sudden and so bright it made everyone in the clearing glance her way, even the demon getting his neck wrung.

The demon that was hit with Ruby's fireball screamed and fell to the forest floor. Its skin started to crack, its bones caving in until there was nothing left.

Ruby panted, shocked. She had never cast something so powerful in the mortal realm before. And it had come so *quickly*, no build-up of warmth, just immediate inferno.

But there was no time for surprise. She turned to the remaining two demons, who had hesitated at her fireball.

"I will give you one chance to retreat," she said gravely.

The pair looked at each other. Then they shrieked and ran at her.

"Ruby," Slate growled.

Ruby concentrated. Flames welled in front of her palms and shot out to coat the demons, who stumbled to their knees and turned into dust.

Just one demon left now. Ruby turned toward the last demon, who was getting its neck crushed in Slate's grip.

The demon clawed at Slate's hands, even as its arms began to crumble.

"*You... betrayed us,*" it choked. "*Supposed to be... guide to lost souls. But you were too busy sleeping. Want... you... to suffer... as we...*"

Slate's fingers closed around a fistful of ash. The demon was dispersed in the wind.

The dog spirit bounded up, barking. It was shockingly loud in the suddenly quiet forest.

"Hush," Ruby told him. "It's all—"

She didn't get a chance to finish. Slate grabbed her shoulders then her chin, twisting her to examine her.

"Are you hurt?" he demanded.

"Am *I* hurt?" She touched his arm, which was still smoking with burns. It had traveled all the way up his black markings and onto the pale skin above his elbow. "Slate, your arm is charcoal!"

"It will heal." Slate cupped her face, his dark eyes boring into hers like he was trying to sense if she was lying about not being hurt. Heat radiated off his palm, his skin crisping against Ruby's cheek.

Slate hissed in pain and dropped her face angrily. "Damned shades."

Ruby stepped toward the shattered remains of the cottage. The net was still lying across it, stopping at the broken stone archway.

"What is that?" Ruby asked, pointing at the flowery net.

Slate ghosted his hand over his burned arm. "Malblossom. It is toxic to Skullstalkers."

"Toxic?" Ruby swallowed. Malblossom rang a bell. Demon hunters kept some in a pouch, just in case. She once overheard one saying he hoped he never had to use it.

She took his arm carefully, wary of the burns from the net and the drying blood from his hunt. "What do we need to do?"

"Nothing." He tugged his arm out of her grip. "It is just my arm. It will heal on its own."

He looked around the broken cottage, his tail lashing. At first, Ruby thought he was glaring at the net. Then she noticed his eyes were strangely soft behind his mask. His shadows were flickering slowly, agitated but not angry. The slow sway looked almost... sad.

Ruby bent down and touched the stacked stones that were once the archway. "What is this place?"

Slate huffed a loud breath through his nose. "This... This was Paimon's. When he was a human."

A cold chill ran down Ruby's spine. She had never heard of this place. It was off the main paths, and no one ever dared venture away from them lest they get stolen by the Bygone.

The dog spirit nudged her hand, pulling her out of her shock. She stroked its head distractedly, struck by the idea that time wasn't as long as she thought, and it was unfolding right in front of her.

"I should have visited him more," Slate said gruffly. "I should have asked him how he was faring. I should have kept an eye on that damn dog."

The dog spirit barked and jumped up at him.

Slate growled, holding his injured arm away from the dog's reach. "Hush! Why do you not call to any of my senses? Why do you have *nowhere* to be?"

The dog spirit licked his burned elbow.

Ruby pulled it away by the scruff, her fingers almost meeting through its ghostly skin. The dog was even less corporeal in this realm. She could hardly see it anymore.

She held the dog firmly and looked up at Slate's burned arm. "We need to clean you up."

"I'll be fine," Slate said. He gave his arm a shake, flicking his own ashy skin to the forest floor.

Ruby grimaced. "I can do it fast. Even if your arm heals, you're covered in blood from your—"

Slate roared. "I said I'll be fine!"

Ruby stepped back, shocked. He had never roared at her like that before. Even in those first days when most things she did annoyed him, he only ever snapped. He never yelled.

The dog spirit whined, its head cocking.

Slate panted, shoulders heaving. For a fearful moment, Ruby thought he might lash out and put his fist through a tree, maybe snap a trunk with his tail.

Then he sagged. His black eyes drifted shut, showing his thin, pale eyelids.

"They were right," he said dully. "I did betray them. Those souls needed me, and I left them to wither into shades because... what? I was busy *sleeping*?"

"You didn't sense them," Ruby tried, stroking the dog spirit so he'd stay calm. "You would have gone to them if you sensed them."

"And yet I didn't." Slate's tail lashed, stirring up leaves. "I am so disconnected from my own void that I didn't sense that somebody had entered it. What kind of guide am I if I let my wanderers rot alone in the forest?"

Ruby couldn't come up with an answer. She had never seen such a mournful sight as Slate, huge and powerful and afraid of nothing, slumping in defeat in the ruins of his old friend's home.

She gathered the dog spirit in her arms, blinking at the strangeness of its near weightlessness. Then she stepped up cautiously beside Slate.

"Come on," she said gently. "Let's get you cleaned up."

Slate glared. But it was a soft glare, and it soon fell to take in the blood drying over his skin. Some of it had baked into the net burns.

He sighed and raised a claw to rip a tear into his void.

"Ah-ah-ah," Ruby said. She batted his hand away. Then, after some thought, she pushed the dog spirit into his arms.

"*I'll* get the portal," she said.

She bent to slide her dagger out of its holster. She expected to find Slate glaring again when she straightened, but when she looked over, he was watching her with something so wondrous her breath stopped in her chest.

FIFTEEN

"That spot is already clean."

Ruby startled and looked down at the patch of chest she had been rubbing with the cloth. It *was* clean, just like the rest of his chest. She had been wiping at it so long the bath water had gone from steaming to lukewarm.

"Just making sure," Ruby said.

She looked up to find him staring at the ceiling, as he had been doing since Ruby settled on his lap and started wiping him down. He had been quiet since they got the dog spirit back home. It had tried to run off into the woods, only for Slate to usher it into the protected castle instead. Ruby occasionally heard paws skittering in the hallway as the dog entertained itself.

Ruby sat up, stretching to scrub his shoulders in a way that exposed her breasts. But Slate didn't bother to watch the bathwater bead around them as she had hoped.

Ruby gave up and laid her chin on his newly cleaned chest. "We're safe. You can stop worrying."

"Safe," he repeated slowly. He shifted, water lapping around them as he moved. "Those demons were lost souls once. They would not have turned if I was watching over this realm as I should."

Ruby bit her lip. It wasn't like she disagreed, but she didn't want him berating himself over it.

"Slate," she tried.

"They were suffering," Slate continued sharply. "I should have been there for them. I am one of the eldest Skullstalkers, and I was given this realm for a *reason*. I cared about helping them, once. I *wanted* to guide them. To show them where they were supposed to be. And now what? Lost souls decay and shrivel into shades while I sleep."

Ruby stroked his ribs, her fingers catching on stray flecks of dried blood she hadn't reached yet.

"You won't bury yourself again," she told him. "Not after they showed you the consequences."

Slate grunted. His lips parted below his mask, and Ruby watched the pink tinge on his teeth. He hadn't washed out his mouth yet.

"You underestimate how long Skullstalkers live," he said quietly. "I am sure I will be an effective guide for a few centuries. But vows fade. *Everything* fades with enough time. Someday I will forget why I cared so much."

The words chilled Ruby to the bone. She knew, logically, that Slate would exist long after she was dead and gone. But to hear him talk about centuries so carelessly...

She swallowed. Even if it was *years* before she could take his knot, it would still be a fraction of his long life. Would he even remember her name in a thousand years?

She tapped his chin. "Lean to the side."

He did. She scrubbed at his neck, then at a stray drop of blood on the hinge of his skull mask that she had missed earlier.

"Will you visit?" she asked, unable to hold it in any longer. "When I go back to my realm."

He fixed his black eyes on her for such a long time that Ruby shrank against him.

She opened her mouth to take it back, but he was already talking.

"If you wish. And I will do my best to keep track of time. So, I don't..." He stopped, his jaw snapping shut so loudly that Ruby jumped.

He stroked her bare back in a silent apology. Water ran down her spine, and Ruby shivered. The water was warm, but his skin was as cool as ever.

"I would hate to lose myself in a dream," he said slowly. "And return to the human realm to find that you died eighty years ago."

Ruby swallowed over a suddenly thick throat. She imagined him a century from now, the sadness fading until he barely remembered why he was sad in the first place. Someday, he would forget everything about her.

She forced a smile. "Maybe my soul will come here after I die."

He sat up, water sloshing over the side of the bath-tub. "*Don't.*"

She blinked, taken aback by the ice in his voice. "What? It could happen. That's one way mortals come into your realm, right? They die with something big unfinished. You could... show me where I'm meant to be."

He shook his head. "I couldn't guide you."

"Why?"

He gazed at her with that dark, intense gaze that never failed to take her breath away.

"Because..." he began, his voice cracking with inhuman hissing.

Then he stopped, his hands coming up to cup her face. He stared at her like he was drinking her in, like he really was about to take that decades-long sleep and wake up to find her gone.

"Because I would want to keep you here," he admitted roughly.

Ruby's heart thundered. He wanted to keep her? Could they even be *together*, when she was a soul without a body? It sounded like a special kind of agony, being near him and never being able to touch him. And yet it meant so much that he said it— even if he was only being sweet, even if he would regret it tomorrow, and even if he would take it back if he actually saw her dead soul walking toward him.

There were a hundred ways this could play out. But for now, she believed him.

She grabbed his skull mask and dragged him down for a kiss.

He surged up, wrapping her in his huge arms. Bone dug into her cheek, and Ruby reveled in it.

She sucked on his tongue. It tasted like blood.

"Fuck me," she begged. "I want you in me. *All* of you."

She wasn't thinking about the ritual. She could only think about his broad chest under her, his cock hardening where she was kneeling above it.

He groaned and tugged her back by her hair. "You can barely manage half."

"I'll make it fit," she promised.

For a minute, she even believed it. He had stretched her last night, and she was still loose enough for him to slide in two fingers. Not to the hilt, but she rode his fingers until she was sitting snug against his palm, his fingers fluttering against that spot that made her gasp.

"I can do it," she breathed. "Give it to me, I can take it."

She reached into the bathwater and gripped his cock. It wasn't as enjoyable underwater since she couldn't feel the slick dripping out his slit, but she rubbed anyway, feeling it harden even further under her touch.

Slate moaned as she ground down determinedly on his fingers. "Patience, little witch. You aren't even wet yet."

She laughed, gesturing at their damp bodies. "I'm wet! I'm the wettest I've ever—*oh*."

Slate smiled, his teeth showing under the mask.

"Not wet enough," he said in a low voice.

Ruby dropped her head against his chest, panting. She had forgotten he only considered her wet after she came at least once.

He slipped a third finger inside her, holding her close as she jerked in his arms.

"Stretching so well for me," he murmured. "So eager to have me inside you."

"Yes," she gasped. She kissed his chest and dug her teeth into his cool skin, wondering if this was how he felt when he pressed his fangs against her: the urge to bite down, to take, to *devour*. She wanted to eat him whole, blunt teeth be damned. She wanted to have him in every way possible.

His smokey eyes met hers. "Brace your hands on the tub."

Ruby grabbed the sides of the bathtub. It was slippery and she ached to touch his chest again, to drag her nails over the bits of blood she hadn't managed to clean off his sides. But she obeyed because she knew what it would get her.

"Very good," Slate purred, thrusting his fingers deep. "Now stay still while you come."

The words vibrated in his throat, sounding like something a creature would say before they pounced out of the dark. It made Ruby wetter every time she heard it.

Her orgasm was coming up on her fast. She wanted to open her mouth, to arch her back. But instead, she locked herself in place, feeling it warm her up from the inside out.

Slate licked her cheek, wrapping his tongue around her throat and squeezing just long enough to pry out a moan, then released.

"Now," Slate told her.

He curled his fingers against her sweet spot. Ruby gripped the sides of the bathtub and came, arms shaking, legs going numb against his powerful thighs.

"There," he said, his voice so thick she barely recognized it. "Now you're wet enough. Stay like that."

He pulled his fingers out, ignoring her pleading whimper.

He held her in place as he lined himself up. Ruby didn't move. He liked her still when he was working his cock into her. *She* liked being held still. It worked very well for both of them.

He pressed his cockhead into her, the shallowest thrust before pulling out. He always started like this, opening her up with small, careful thrusts until he was properly inside.

Ruby dug her teeth into her lip until it stung. She loved how carefully he fucked her. That he never truly hurt her when he could do it so easily. But she wanted him to *stop* being careful. To fuck her with complete abandon. To shove himself inside entirely, not work himself halfway in and stop himself from pushing deeper.

They both sighed as the head pressed in.

"Yeah," Ruby said, barely holding herself back from rocking her hips. "Just like that. Give me more?"

"Just who is in charge here, little witch?" Slate asked, his black eyes gleaming with mirth. Something was underneath it, something intent and tender that took her breath away. Then she squeezed around him, and his eyes went half-lidded.

"Good question," Ruby said. "If you aren't going to fuck me properly, maybe I should—*ohhh*!"

She cut off with a cry on the next thrust. It was faster than he would usually allow, giving her less time to adjust before he went deeper. She could feel her inner walls stretching to accommodate him, always straining no matter how many times they did this.

Slate grabbed her hips, holding her still as he fucked deeper. Water splashed out over the sides of the tub. Ruby's arms trembled as she braced herself.

"Taking me so well," Slate groaned.

Ruby moaned. He was so big. *Impossibly* big. She couldn't take any more.

She looked down. He had only worked half his cock inside. His knot sat under the bathwater, thick and tantalizing.

She gritted her teeth. "Keep going."

Slate's hips faltered. "It will not fit."

"I'll *make* it fit!" Ruby bore down, wincing as it immediately started to sting. And it wasn't just the sting: she could feel her inner walls protesting, could feel his cock bump up against the end of her hole.

Slate gripped her hips hard, stilling her.

"I cannot go any deeper," he said reluctantly. "I can feel your end. I know you can feel it, too."

"But..." Ruby's eyes pricked. "You said..."

Slate kissed her, his tongue curling against the roof of her mouth.

"I will consult my brothers," he assured her. "You have opened for me this much. There must be a way to open you more."

He lifted her up and nudged her back down, the movement inside her making Ruby moan. But it wasn't enough: it was too much, as always. But still not *enough*. It wouldn't be enough until she felt those powerful hips snapping against her, his knot swelling inside her.

"I don't want you to consult anyone," she said, rocking against him. "I want all of you. The ward ritual—"

Slate's fingers dug into her thighs. "Don't think about that."

"But—"

He grabbed her chin. His grip was firm, but the claw he stroked over her cheek was so gentle.

"Just let yourself feel it," he urged. "Doesn't it feel good?"

Ruby wanted to protest. To point out that this was all for nothing if she couldn't make him fit. That even if the ward magically fixed itself tomorrow, she still needed it. She needed it in a way she didn't fully understand, a need that went deeper than anything she had ever felt. She needed his knot like she needed air or food, and she couldn't believe she could have gone her whole life without knowing that.

But he was fucking into her faster now, and her words trailed off in a frustrated moan. Then he reached for her clit, and everything melted except his huge cock and his big, careful finger rubbing circles over her nub.

"Your task right now is not to take all of me," he rumbled. "Your task is to come on my cock. Can you do that, little witch?"

Ruby couldn't talk beyond a series of panting moans. She nodded instead, her eyes squeezing shut as he pounded faster.

"Good," Slate said raggedly. His fingers tightened around her jaw. "*Come.*"

Ruby came with a cry, wave after wave of pleasure crashing over her as he fucked her through it.

"Glorious," Slate said, his voice deep and guttural. "Open your eyes, little witch. Look at me while I fill you up."

Ruby pried her eyes open. They were watery with tears, but she could see his slack mouth as he moved faster inside her. His tongue was lolling out, the tip grazing her nipple with every thrust.

Slate grunted, half feral. "Say my name."

Ruby let out a small, overwhelmed sob. "*Slate.*"

Slate growled. A claw dug hard into her cheek, nearly piercing the skin as his hips stilled, pouring hot ropes of come deep inside.

Ruby's mouth dropped open, her eyelids fluttering. It was so good she almost forgot that half his cock was still sticking out of her, throbbing with each pulse. She looked down to watch his knot swell under the bathwater, her hole throbbing with want even as he filled her.

His growl faded into a spent moan. He tucked her head into his chest, and they sat there for a long minute, breathing in tandem.

Ruby shifted. His cock was soft inside her now, and she could feel the first round of his slick dripping out. This was usually a sign that he would start up again, pushing himself deeper.

Instead, he lifted her off of him. She made a noise of protest as he slipped out of her, and he shushed her.

"We came in here to get clean," he reminded her. "We did not do very well."

Ruby laughed shakily. When he held up a cloth, she let him wipe her salt-streaked cheeks.

By the time he had finished wiping them both down, Ruby was sagging against him.

He picked her up in his arms, cradling her to his chest.

She made a sleepy noise against his nipple. "I can take it again."

"Not tonight." He curled his tail around her ankle and gave her a comforting squeeze. "Tonight, you will rest."

She tried to complain. But the day had been so exhausting, and he was carrying her so gently that when he lowered her onto the castle bed, she was already half in a dream.

She still managed to grab his horn as he went to pull away.

"Want your nest," she mumbled. "Want... want to wake up with you."

First, there was nothing. Then lips pressed against her forehead. The slightest pinch of a bone mask pressed with it.

"Goodnight," Slate said quietly. "Little witch."

Sixteen

This was usually when Slate retreated to his nest. But it was getting harder to leave his mortal after they had completed their stretching sessions.

He sighed, smoothing her long, dark hair away from her face. Then he pressed a kiss to the mark he had dented into her cheek with his skull mask and got up.

"I will be back before you wake," he whispered.

He paused at the door, watching her chest rise and fall. He had remembered to place the covers over her this time. Mortals were so sensitive to the cold.

The portal only burned for a minute before Wick stepped into his void.

"Slate," he said, his fiery eyes flickering with surprise as he stepped into the shadowy forest. "I did not expect to see you again so soon. How was the kobald?"

"Fine." Slate licked his back teeth, where flecks of demon flesh still clung.

Wick nodded, looking pleased. Another thing Slate appreciated about him: he seemed honestly excited by others' happiness.

"It is good to see you hunting again," Wick told him. "I thought your fangs had dulled."

Slate snorted. "You would know."

Wick's wings twitched. His eyes flamed even as he looked away, and Slate wondered if there had been another incident of blood frenzy. Wick had been careful to stay away from situations that triggered it, but there was no escape.

Slate opened his mouth to apologize, but Wick talked over him, alarmed.

"What happened to your arm? That was not the kobald."

Slate raised his burned arm. "Malblossom. My attackers regretted it."

"May you heal fast." Wick bowed his head. "I'm glad you summoned me. I wanted to speak with you."

Slate frowned. "You did? About what?"

Wick hesitated. "How goes training the human?"

"Fine," Slate lied. Then he stopped, his tail lashing. "When you mated with them. How did you make yourself fit?"

Wick made a considering noise that sounded like flames crackling. "Mm. About that... I may have been exaggerating about mating with mortals."

"What?" Slate barked. He imagined going back to

Ruby and telling her that actually they couldn't fulfill the ritual, that she would have to find some other magic-using creature to mate with her. "You said you could do it!"

"I've heard others say that, but *I'm* not dumb enough to—" Wick stopped, coughing ash into his fist. "I mean, they are *very* small."

Slate growled, grinding his fangs together. That wasn't so much of a problem for Wick, who was smaller than him. Most Skullstalkers were.

"*But*," Wick said desperately. "That doesn't mean it's impossible. I was asking around, and there is a spell—"

"Show me," Slate demanded.

Wick's wings twitched apologetically. "It is in the mortal realm. There's a cave deep in the moors of Anderfel where one of our brothers resides."

Slate grabbed his hand and straightened it into a claw, pointing it into the forest air.

"Focus on it," he ordered.

Wick made a rumbling noise of confusion. But his fiery eyes drifted shut, and Slate channeled his power into him.

Wick's wings flexed, his flaming eyes flashing open in shock as Slate used his finger to draw a portal in the cool forest air.

"*Oh*," Wick whispered. He stared at the portal in disbelief, examining the flickering white hole in the middle of the forest. "I have never done that before."

"And you will not again," Slate said. He dropped

Wick's hand. "Come with me. If I am to encounter another Skullstalker, I may need to fight."

Wick said nothing. For a moment, Slate thought he might have offended him, which was ridiculous. However Wick felt about his blood frenzy, it was useful sometimes.

Wick's eyes focused on the distance as if he was remembering something he thought he'd forgotten. His eyes sparked, and Slate extended his claws even further than usual. He'd seen those eyes flicker that hard before; it was the only time he was truly afraid of his brother.

Then Wick blinked, and he was the mild-mannered Skullstalker Slate knew.

"Lead," Wick said, turning to face the glowing white hole in the middle of Slate's void. "I will follow."

They stepped through the portal into a forest so dark that even Slate had to let his eyes adjust.

"Humans don't venture here often," Wick explained as Slate sealed the portal behind them. "For obvious reasons."

Slate grunted. The darkness was so intense it swirled around him, thicker and heavier than the shadows in his own void.

He peered through the forest. He could hardly see the trees ahead of him, which stunk of sulfur. But he could see a tiny light in the distance.

"There," Wick announced. "That's the cave."

Slate was thankful that Wick had placed them so

close to it. If someone got distracted while making a portal, they could end up days away from their destination.

Shadows parted around them as they walked, dragging on their skin. Slate could feel his own darkness spasming around his skull mask, batting away the new shadows.

A gruff voice echoed through the dark. "Ho there, brothers. What brings you to this strange place?"

The lights ahead of them multiplied. It wasn't a torch like Slate had assumed. They were eyes, beaming through the darkness.

Their surroundings came into sharper view with each step. By the time Slate arrived in front of the Skullstalker, he could see the cave behind him, huge and cavernous.

The Skullstalker looked... old. Older than Slate, which was impossible. He knew all his older siblings, and this was not one of them. But he couldn't find another explanation for the chipped, aged bone over his face, or his cloudy eyes, or the skin sagging off his limbs.

He was dressed in odd human clothes, bones hanging from a chain around his neck. They all looked like jawbones, but the teeth were nothing Slate recognized.

"Brothers," the Skullstalker said, his voice so quiet Slate had to lean in to hear it. "I welcome you into my void."

"This is not a void," Slate pointed out. "You are in the mortal realm."

"My void-away-from-void, then." The Skullstalker's black eyes glittered. "What do you wish of me?"

The words were a surprise. Skullstalkers were not a helpful species. Other than Wick, who was an exception to the rule. This Skullstalker's voice might be soft, and his skin was sallow with age, but Slate was still fighting the urge to crouch in preparation for a fight.

"I have a mortal," he said slowly. "I need to... fit inside."

He expected surprise. Or at the very least, amused laughter. But the Skullstalker only bowed his head, a shocking risk when encountering two unknowns. The back of his neck was completely exposed.

"We can do that," the Skullstalker said plainly. "Come with me."

He turned and walked toward the cave. His gait was slow, almost a waddle. Slate exchanged a confused look with Wick, who looked back like he expected Slate to tell him what to do next.

The Skullstalker twisted to beckon him in. "There are no gnashing jaws waiting to devour you. Come."

Slate took a cautious step toward the cavern, tail swishing suspiciously. "I will stay. Whatever is required, I will do it from here."

He waited for the Skullstalker to stop, for his eyes to gleam threateningly. For the Skullstalker's lips to peel back from his fangs and a snarl to rip through the cave.

But the Skullstalker only waved a dismissive hand, barely visible in the gloom. "The oil is not heavy. I can deliver it to you."

"Oil?" Wick whispered beside him.

Slate didn't answer. Wick's magic was so weak it

might as well not exist, and he did not study theory. It made sense he would not know much about anointing oil.

The Skullstalker shuffled back into view carrying a pot of black oil. He dipped a finger in, grunting with effort as his claws retracted. It took several seconds longer than expected for the claw to slide back into his hand.

He pressed his dripping finger against Slate's skull. Slate tried to pay attention to the patterns, but they were strange and nothing he recognized.

"What will this do?" Slate demanded.

The Skullstalker hummed, smoothing a line over his collarbones. "When you push into her, her body will shift to make room for you."

Lust curled in Slate's stomach as he imagined sinking into Ruby's hole all the way to the hilt. Feeling her body clench, his cock nudging the end of her wall, then feeling it *stretch*—

He forced the lust down and met the Skullstalker's cloudy eyes. "Will it harm her?"

"No. But the spell will consume a portion of your essence."

"Slate," Wick whispered.

"Essence," Slate repeated, sending Wick a look to quiet him. "What do you mean by this?"

"Your magic will weaken. And you will age faster."

His heart raced. "How fast?"

"You would only have a few millennia left."

A few millennia. Slate fought down a shocking wave of disappointment. Part of him had hoped—just for a moment—that it would narrow his lifespan to a truly pitiful amount of time.

Like a human lifespan.

"That seems a steep cost," Wick said. "Slate. Are you sure this mortal is worth it?"

Slate didn't look at him. He was thinking back to Ruby asleep in that castle bed. How she had asked for his nest before she fell asleep.

"She has bound me," he said. "I must complete the warding ritual, as is her wish."

The Skullstalker hummed, interested. "A binding? What will you have of her when the ward is complete?"

Slate frowned. "Does it matter?"

The Skullstalker smiled, exposing several missing fangs. "I talk to so few people. Let alone, my brothers. Indulge me with stories beyond this forest."

Slate shifted uncomfortably. He didn't want to talk about this, least of all with two brothers listening. But the Skullstalker was granting him a great boon so he could, at least, provide him an answer.

"I want her to stay," he admitted, his voice raw. "I want to *make* her stay."

The Skullstalker rumbled as he ran a black line down Slate's chest. "And will you?"

"I... don't know." Slate averted his gaze to the huge, formless darkness of the cave. "She cares for her town. For her realm. Even though they have given her no reason to."

His fists clenched with rage as he thought back to the vapid townsfolk he had overheard talking of Ruby. His sweet, stubborn witch, doing all this work for people who didn't appreciate her.

The Skullstalker stepped back, admiring his work. "Are you ready?"

"Do it," Slate said quietly.

The Skullstalker hummed. One claw came back out, the movement jerky with effort. He pricked their palms and dripped blood into the jar of oil. Then he painted one last mark onto Slate's lower lip.

The Skullstalker lowered his head. He mumbled something low under his breath, the words reverberating through the cave and making both Slate and Wick shiver.

Whatever language it was, Slate didn't know it. But it sounded old, and it had the short, clicking syllables he remembered from his early existence before he had a void.

Something tingled deep inside Slate's groin as the Skullstalker spoke. Then it expanded, spreading until his claw tips were resonating with it.

The Skullstalker fell silent. The tingle stopped, and Slate realized he was sweating. He stumbled back, falling into Wick, who chirped in shock and grabbed him.

"What have you done?" Slate repeated, struggling back up. "If it is anything other than what I asked—"

"I have done what you wanted, brother," the Skullstalker assured him. "When you mate with her, her body will oblige. There will be no pain and no damage."

Slate wanted to sag with relief. But he had already embarrassed himself by falling into Wick, who was watching Slate with a concern that both touched and annoyed him.

Slate straightened, ignoring the heaviness weighing his bones down. He felt weary in a way that sleep would not cure.

"I owe you a boon," he said.

The Skullstalker waved another dismissive claw. "I do not keep track. I would ask you to return someday and tell me the next chapter of your story, as determined by my spell."

"I will," Slate promised. "And if you are ever in need, my void is open to you."

The Skullstalker bowed once more. It seemed to take him great effort to straighten again.

"I do not leave very often," the Skullstalker said. "But... the offer is appreciated."

Slate turned to leave. Wick stayed still, watching the Skullstalker rub a cloth over his oily hands.

"Brother," Wick said beseechingly.

But Wick wasn't talking to him, he was still watching the Skullstalker.

The Skullstalker didn't look up as he answered, "Yes?"

Wick rubbed the edge of his wing worriedly. "Is there... is there anything you can do for me? I am—"

"I know what you are." The Skullstalker glanced up, a hint of genuine sorrow in his cloudy eyes. "The frenzy is nothing I can cure. It is in you, as deep as your bones."

Wick stared at him, his jaw tightening. His fiery eyes flared, his wings snapping out, and Slate readied himself to leap on him. Wick asked so little of him, except to hold him back if the frenzy started.

Then Wick's wings drooped. The fire in his eyes dimmed.

"Okay," Wick said softly. "Thanks, anyhow."

Slate waited. Wick walked back to him, so drooping and dejected that for a moment Slate could not imagine him hurting anyone.

Then Wick looked up, and his fiery eyes glinted. Slate was reminded of an old Skullstalker saying he had not heard in hundreds of years: *a beast is a beast is a beast.*

They stepped through the glowing portal into a pile of dripping black leaves.

Slate breathed a sigh of relief as he took in the familiar shadowy trees. He was genuine in his offer to the Skullstalker, but he had no urge to visit that place ever again. He would, of course, return to tell him the story as he wished. But depending on how things ended with Ruby, he would give it a hundred years or so for the bitterness to leave his words.

He turned to Wick. "Thank you for bringing me to that place. I owe you a boon, too."

"I will keep that in mind." Wick gave him a half-hearted smile, not bothering to keep his lips over his fangs in case Slate thought it was a threat.

"How do you feel?" Wick continued.

Slate rotated his shoulders. He still felt weak. It was fading fast, but there was a noticeable heaviness to his bones that wasn't fading. He wondered if it was permanent.

"Diminished," he replied honestly. "But it will be worth it."

He started toward the castle. His mind was so consumed with thoughts of Ruby he didn't realize he had forgotten something until Wick called, "Brother."

Slate turned to find Wick standing uncomfortably among his trees. He opened his mouth to tell Wick to stop standing there and open a portal already, only to remember that his brother was useless with magic.

Slate headed back, claw raised. "Where do you wish to be?"

"The mortal realm," Wick replied. "Where you summoned me from."

Slate's nose wrinkled behind his skull mask as he cut a circle into the air. "Every time I visit, the air feels more stale. It does not want us there. I don't know why you prefer it."

"Some do," Wick said softly.

Slate's claw paused in midair, a mere inch away from completing the portal. He thought back to Ruby speaking of her town with such fondness, even if there was sadness in it. Of her delight whenever he brought her something from that realm that his barren void could never provide.

He finished the circle. The portal sealed and started to glow, pulsing in wait.

Wick stepped toward it and paused. "Good luck, brother."

Slate watched him step into the portal. His wings were still drooping, his fiery eyes dull with disappointment. Slate did not understand why his brother was so upset about his blood frenzy, but he sympathized. It must be a heavy burden, carrying something inside you that you hated.

"Brother," he said. He waited until Wick looked back, half of him shimmering beyond the portal.

Slate inclined his head. "May your fangs be dull."

Wick huffed, tail swishing sadly. "We can only hope."

Then he vanished through the portal, leaving Slate to seal it behind him.

He scratched at the oil drying on his face. He would have to wash it off. And then...

He looked into the forest. His nest wasn't far. He had time.

Seventeen

Ruby woke up to something warm and wet touching her cheek.

She opened her eyes. Slate was bending over the bed, his tongue pulling away from her face.

She squinted at him. "Did you just... *lick* me?"

"You were taking a very long time to wake up," Slate replied. "I was worried. So was the dog."

The dog spirit scratched at the door with a mournful whine.

"You will not be let in," Slate called. "Shoo."

There was another sad bark, followed by the sound of the spirit slinking away.

Ruby laughed. It quickly trailed off as she realized what was surrounding them.

It wasn't bedsheets like she thought. It was fur.

Fur and feathers. But no dirt, like she was used to smelling when she was in his forest nest. This nest was full of sweetness and softness; literal sweetness, she realized as she spotted wrapped chocolate tucked next to a shadowy feather.

She sat up, staring around the bedroom. The only thing remaining of her bed was several pillows tucked around her. The rest was all nest, complete with leaves and dark spiderwebs.

"Gods," she whispered, overwhelmed.

"I cannot sleep without it," Slate said quickly. "I can remove it if you wish."

He started to rise. She grabbed him, pulling him back down into the nest with her.

"No! This is good. This is..." She looked around, letting out a disbelieving giggle. "This is *incredible*. Is this going to stay here?"

"For as long as you wish."

She stared at him, amazed. She had a fuzzy memory of asking for his nest last night, but she hadn't thought he would actually *do* anything about it. The idea that he'd done it on some mumbled, sleepy request made her heart turn over in her chest.

She rubbed the edge of his skull mask fondly. "What about your forest? You've been sleeping in it since before my town was founded."

"Long before," Slate agreed. He wrapped an arm around her cautiously, as if he was waiting to be rebuffed. "The forest is still there. But... *you* are here."

Ruby's eyes burned. She ducked her head, breathing in the heady scent of fur. "I would have come to your nest in the forest."

"I wanted to make a new one." Slate twisted his tail,

sweeping it over the massive nest they were curled up in. "Do you like it?"

Ruby looked around again at the soft furs and chocolates tucked into the lining.

"I do," she said. "Thank you. For staying."

She pressed her face into his neck, trying to hide her burning eyes. Slate rubbed her back, but there was something hesitant in his touch.

Ruby pulled back. Slate's black eyes were wide behind his bone mask, his tail swishing anxiously.

Ruby frowned. "Slate? What is it?"

"I have something for you," he admitted.

Ruby tensed at his serious tone. She sat up, clutching a layer of fur over her bare chest. "What is it?"

Slate hesitated. "You cannot naturally fit me. Your mortal body is too small."

Ruby shrank into herself. She could feel his come dripping out of her swollen hole onto the fur below them. He hadn't cleaned it up with his tongue like he often did.

"I can do it," she insisted. "If we just—"

He cut her off. "There are limits. We have both felt them."

Ruby flushed, averting her eyes. "I had limits the first time, and we worked on them! I *know* I can do it."

Slate shushed her, pulling her into his lap.

Ruby steadied herself against his chest, her eyes stinging. "Are you... telling me it's useless? Are you telling me to *leave*?"

It didn't make sense. He *just* made her a nest. Maybe this was his way of saying goodbye?

"No," Slate assured her. His tongue slid over her red cheek, nudging the corners of her eyes where tears were starting to well.

He was being *very* touchy, Ruby considered as he ran his hands up her bare back. If he hoped that would make it easier to let her down like this, he had something else coming.

But before she could insist they keep trying, Slate spoke again.

"I have sought out a spell," he said. "It has diminished me. But it will allow me to fit inside of you."

Ruby stilled, her mind racing. Diminished?

"Do you mean it made you..." Ruby sat back, eyeing his loincloth underneath her hips. "Smaller?"

"No." Slate nuzzled her neck, breathing in her scent. "It will rearrange your body. While I am inside you, anyhow."

The revelation shot through her, leaving glowing red embers in its place. Ruby knew she should be horrified. Part of her *was* horrified, imagining organs and muscles moving to make way for his giant cock.

She pulled back. "Will it hurt?"

"No!" Slate growled, dragging her closer until she was crushed against him. "It is painless. When I am finished, your body will return to how it once was."

"Oh." Ruby let the realization wash over her. It felt like something physical, like water dripping over her head and down her body.

She could have all of him. She could have what she had wanted since the first time he bent her over the ward stone. She could feel him fuck into her as deep and rough as he wanted, no need to hold back. She could have his hips flush against her, his knot stretching her until they locked together.

And then she would leave. Would she ever have him inside her again? Would he even want her ten years from now, or forty? Would he slip into a decades-long slumber by accident and wake up to find her long gone, just like he feared?

"Mortal," Slate said quietly. "*Ruby*."

Ruby looked up at him. He was watching her. Waiting for her response, she realized.

He rubbed idly at her naked thighs. He was so close to her puffy entrance, still leaking his slick. Come dripped out of her and onto his loincloth, onto the nest he had constructed around her while she slept. He would have had to lift her so delicately to place her onto this mountain of furs.

Ruby watched his come pool out of her. Suddenly all the devastation at the idea of never feeling him again was gone, replaced by a fiery need that almost made her giddy. They could do it. They could really, *truly* do it. Whatever came next, they still had this.

She flung her arms around his neck and kissed him, running her tongue over his fangs.

He made a muffled noise against her and pulled back. "I will take you to the anointing room."

He wrapped her legs around him and started to lift her.

She kicked him in the back. "No! Let's - let's test it first."

Slate faltered. "Are you sure?"

"Yes," Ruby said instantly. There was a small voice in the back of her head reminding her that if the ward failed when they could be completing the ritual to renew it, the deaths of her entire town would be on her head. But it was easy to ignore. The ward had been failing for months, it was not as if it would suddenly break if they put off the ritual for another twenty minutes.

She kissed him deeper, sucking on his impossibly long tongue until it threatened to choke her. She made an incoherent noise, which he translated correctly by throwing her onto her back among the furs.

He crawled down her body, kissing and nipping at her bare skin. She closed her eyes, wishing that his fangs would press harder and finally break the skin. She wanted a mark. A ropey scar. Anything to prove that her time here had been real.

He kissed her navel. She imagined a thick blue line painted over it and shivered hungrily. Soon she would be anointed, a construct of a spell made to be plowed and used. But for now—

"You don't need to start with that," she reminded him breathily as his long, dripping tongue circled her entrance. "You can just use your cock."

He raised his head, his black eyes incredulous.

"Where exactly is the fun in that?" he demanded. Then he pushed his tongue inside her in one long slide.

They both moaned in shock as his tongue kept going. Usually, he could only fit half of it, just like his cock. But it kept sliding inside her, in and in and *in*.

Ruby gasped in amazement. She could feel him all the way in her torso. She could even feel her insides moving, sliding in a way that should have frightened her. But instead, it just made her feel... hot. She had spent so much time wishing for more of him, and now she was getting it. No matter what had to move to make him fit.

His nose brushed her clit, and Ruby jerked. His mouth rested against her entrance, his tongue inside her all the way to the root.

"*Gods*," Ruby moaned. "You're so *big*."

Slate groaned against her, the noise vibrating through her clit. He started to tongue-fuck her in earnest, last night's come squelching out around him. She felt him seal his lips around her entrance and suck, and her hips bucked involuntarily at the incredible pressure.

"I can feel you so deep," she groaned. "Gods, Slate, give me your cock. I want to feel it."

Slate rumbled and grabbed her waist. He started to bounce her, pulling her onto his tongue and then sliding her back off. Up and down, the nest's fur sliding against her naked back.

He made her come like that, gripping the nest and wailing. He didn't slow down as she sagged against the bed, shaking with exertion.

"I want your cock," she babbled as he kept licking into her. "I want it, please give it to me, *ohhhh*—"

He pulled his tongue from her with a slick pop. His eyes raised to meet hers, glittering black.

"Is this not enough?" he rasped. "You're trembling."

"I want it." Ruby stroked his horns, trailing from the points to the ends where the horn became skin. "It's everything we've been working up to. I've worked so hard, Slate, please... please give me my reward."

Slate's jaw snapped shut as he growled. He blurred up her body and hooked his arms under her knees. His eyes never left her face, even as he lined himself up against her entrance.

"Little witch," he said simply.

Then he shoved in. There was no careful working the head in, no minuscule thrusts working himself inside. Just one hard thrust, so long and deep they both cried out in shock.

Ruby gripped his shoulders, her arms straining with the width. It was nothing compared to the strain inside her: she could feel her body adjusting yet again, every-thing sliding and expanding to make room for his enor-mous length.

She looked down and whimpered. He was all the way inside her...

Almost.

His knot sat against her entrance, tight and starting to swell. They both groaned as he ground against her.

"You are so tight," Slate said roughly. His hands spasmed around her legs. "How does it feel?"

Ruby tried to answer. Then his hips hitched, and whatever she was about to say cut off in a shocked groan. She craned her head again to watch it happen, his hips barely sliding out before fucking back into her again.

He was *huge*. He had been right: there was no way a mortal could have taken him. Not without magical help.

Ruby thanked the gods for whatever spell had allowed this and kissed his chest, the only part of him she could reach.

Slate bent down, curling hard so he could kiss her mouth.

"Ruby," he mumbled as he fucked her. "Little witch. Mortal. *Mine*."

"Yours," Ruby gasped, her eyes growing damp with it. She could barely move, too lost in the feeling of his impossible cock moving inside her. She was going to come again; she could feel it within every inch of her.

Slate's hips worked faster, jarring her up the bed.

"Again," he begged. "Say it again."

"I'm yours," Ruby managed.

Slate snarled against her mouth, the sound trailing off in a desperate whine. His hips shoved forward with more force than ever, and Ruby yelled in triumph as she felt his knot squeeze into her.

Slate stilled. His mouth opened on a roar as he spilled inside her, each hot pulse sending Ruby closer and closer to the edge until she fell over with him.

Her vision greyed out. When she came to, he was panting on top of her. Her hole was stretched around his knot, which throbbed in time with her heartbeat.

Slate huffed against her hair. "I... I will last longer during the ritual."

Ruby laughed. The vibration made Slate groan, his soft cock twitching weakly inside her.

Ruby shifted happily. She ached, even with the magic smoothing the way. She would be surprised if she would be able to walk without a limp tomorrow. But she had never felt so complete as Slate gathered her in his arms and kissed her, his knot locking them together in the warm center of his nest.

EIGHTEEN

I would never sleep again if I got to have this, Slate thought as he rolled onto his back, careful not to dislodge his knot. *I would stay awake for the rest of time to make sure I never missed a second.*

Ruby made a shocked noise as she settled above him, as if she couldn't believe his knot was really inside her. Then she braced her hands on his stomach, her hips moving in tiny motions against the knot.

He grabbed her hips, stilling them. "Careful. I will get hard again before we make it to the ward stone."

"How awful," Ruby teased. She rocked again, squirming against his hard hold.

Slate's smile dimmed. The ritual was so close. Then she would be gone from him. He would visit, of course. But she would be gone so fast. Eighty years was barely a blink for a Skullstalker. No, she was almost thirty—only *fifty* years to go. The concept was indescribable.

Ruby dug her teeth into her lip. "You could anoint me while you're still inside me. No need to stay soft."

Slate's anguish over her leaving vanished into lust as he imagined it: lying her out on the tiles, their bodies still joined as he smoothed blue oil over her naked chest.

"I could carry you," he said slowly.

She nodded eagerly.

Slate gripped her thighs and stood. She yelped, the sound turning into a moan as his knot tugged at her inner walls.

"Gods," she whispered. "That's so good. I never knew *anything* could feel this good. I'm never going to get used to it."

Slate stopped. He looked down just in time to see her pleased smile turn stiff.

"I mean," she started. "It... will be difficult to settle for mortal men."

Her words filled Slate with bitterness. For a moment, he almost wished the mortal had left him to his slumber. He could have slept another century and never known she existed. Instead, he would be left with an empty realm frequented only by lost souls he was bound to fail as the centuries passed.

Maybe there will be another mortal, he thought. The thought made his stomach curdle. There was no other mortal. Only Ruby. Ruby and her sweet, stubborn nature, her kindness and her curiosity, and her eager, tight cunt.

There would never be another. Slate had never loved before this. He would never love again. It was a harrowing realization to have when he was still inside her, his knot binding them together in the nest he had constructed around her while she slept.

"Slate?"

Slate startled. He had been making a low, mournful whine without realizing it.

He cut himself off and nodded. "I will take you to the anointing oil."

He walked her there slowly, through every twisting hall she had started mapping out in those first few weeks.

She stayed silent, for the most part. A few whimpers when he readjusted her, a gasp or two when his hips twitched against his will. But mostly she was quiet, her cheek pressed into his chest and her hands on his shoulders.

Finally, Slate led them into the bathroom where he had first anointed her. The jar of blue liquid remained, with traces of liquid dried to the floor where they had dripped off her body.

Slate held her close, considering.

"Hold still," he told her. Then he knelt and lowered her carefully to the floor, propping her hips up on his legs.

He leaned back. She looked delectable, laid out like this, with her hole stretched out around his knot.

He traced the place where they were joined, making them both hiss.

"Don't get distracted," she reminded him with a grin.

"*I* wanted to go to the stone ward," he replied. He took the jar and set it next to her head. Then he dipped his fingers to the hilt.

Ruby stayed still as he wound lines around her breasts, her navel, and her neck. She didn't look away once, her breath slow and even as she watched him paint her. Slate couldn't help but think back to the first time they had done this, her breath quick and panicked, how she had trembled under his touch.

There was some trembling. But he could recognize it for what it was: aftershocks of the pleasure he'd given her. Mortals were, after all, so very responsive.

He finished with her lower lip. He left one dark spot, tugging it down until her lips parted.

She blinked up at him very slowly, her lip dragging against his finger.

Slate let his finger drop away and sat back. She was so beautiful like this, covered in his markings, her dark hair clouding around her head and her eyes fixed on his.

Her tongue darted out to brush over the spot he'd painted on her lip. "What is it?"

Slate didn't know what to say. *You're the most beautiful thing I've ever seen. You've made me feel more awake than anything in all my long existence. Don't leave.*

"You look like you deserve to be worshipped," he said instead.

He carried her to the stone ward next. It took a long

time, and they were both panting when they finally emerged into the forest clearing.

Slate adjusted her on his newly hard cock. His knot had deflated on the walk, and he had to force himself not to shove her against a tree and rut until he finished again.

He laid her out on the stone slab, right over the faint blue glow of the rune.

"Are you ready?" he asked.

She stared up at him, chest heaving. The paint was smudged, but the lines were still there. It would work.

He thought sadly of breaking one of those lines with his thumb so the spell would fail. Then he saw the heady determination in her eyes and stopped himself.

She pulled on his horns. "Do it. Fuck me."

Only if you stay, he thought. *We are bound; I can* make *you stay.*

He didn't say it. Instead, he pulled back, slamming back into her with such force they both yelled.

"Gods," she whined. She threw her head back, sliding her hands down to cover his hands where they were holding her legs back. "I'm going to bruise tomorrow."

Slate fucked into her again, grinding his hips against her. "Do you wish me to be gentle?"

"No," she gasped. "I-I want you to take me as hard as you can. Don't hold back."

He knew he shouldn't listen to her. She was so fragile. But he couldn't stop himself. He shoved harder inside, letting the bulb of his thickening knot catch against her entrance.

Ruby gasped. Her hands flew down to touch her

stomach, where a bulge appeared every time he bottomed out.

They both groaned as she covered the spot with her hands. He couldn't feel her fingers through her skin, but he could feel how deep she was letting him in. He could feel his own spend dripping around him, could feel her body stretch and strain to accommodate that as well. And yet she was still so *tight*. As if the spell stretched her to barely fit him, but no more.

The clearing filled with the wet sounds of mating, their ragged cries climbing to join it.

Slate bent over her, fucking her so hard the stone ward rocked on the ground. Then he caught a glimpse of stray wetness on her cheek and stopped.

Ruby whimpered. "Don't stop!"

He let his tongue drop out, licking up the salt. "You're weeping."

Ruby opened her wet eyes. Another tear ran down the side of her face, blurring—but not breaking—the lines on her cheek.

"It feels so good," she said thickly. "I-I can't believe this is happening. *Please* don't stop, Slate. I want to be yours."

Slate groaned and buried himself as deep as he could go, watching her belly bulge with it. He bent down and caught her mouth in a vicious kiss, his fangs catching her lip.

The ritual paint stayed intact. But when he drew back, there was a smudge imprinted on his own mouth.

Mine, Slate thought.

He growled and came, hot come gushing deep inside. He shoved his knot as deep as he could, legs quaking as he swelled and locked them together.

Ruby cried out, arching against the slab. "*Yes!*"

Blue light radiated from her hair. Slate lifted his head groggily, watching. For a moment he thought that *she* was glowing. Then he saw Paimon's rune below her and understood.

The ritual was working. He could feel magic filling the air, sharp and electric. The symbol underneath Ruby glowed brighter until she was backlit by a sea of blue.

Ruby didn't seem to notice. Her eyes were squeezed shut, and her hands locked around his horns as he fucked into her.

In the distance, the dog spirit barked.

Ruby gasped. Her eyes flew open, and Slate startled.

Blue light flowed out of Ruby's eyes and streamed down her cheeks. Light climbed her skin and her hair, turning each dark thread ward-blue.

Slate panicked, grabbing Ruby's shoulders. "Ruby!"

But Ruby was still arching, her hands still locked around his horns. She wasn't in pain, he realized as the light grew so bright Slate's dark eyes watered. She was coming, he could feel her squeezing around his cock.

Finally, the light began to dim. Ruby sagged against the stone slab, her chest heaving. She was giggling faintly.

He stroked her hair out of her face, relieved and torn. They had done it. His part of their binding was fulfilled. Her town was safe—

A loud crack rang out through the clearing.

Slate stared as a fissure appeared in the stone above Ruby's head.

"Ruby," he said.

Ruby didn't move. She was staring up at the evening sky, her face set in a wide grin.

Another crack split the stone underneath Ruby's hips.

"*Ruby*," Slate snapped. He went to scoop her up, only to stop when Ruby's hand slapped into his chest.

"Don't," she said.

Slate reeled. There was something in her voice, old and oddly familiar.

"Your ward," he said, panicked. "It isn't renewing. It's breaking. I do not understand what we did wrong."

Ruby's hand gentled, rubbing over his chest.

"We did nothing wrong," she said. "But we need to go."

She looked down to where they were joined, her expression turning mournful. Then she reached down and slid her fingertip over the spot where they were joined.

Slate jerked. His knot was shrinking. The cause was magical, he could feel it surging through him.

"Ruby," he whispered. "I don't—"

She shushed him. Then she leaned up, kissing him long and deep as his knot softened and the stone ward cracked into tiny pieces behind them.

"Let me down," she said.

Bewildered, he did. He looked around the woods, checking for demons who might be playing another cruel trick. But he could sense no one. Just him and Ruby, alone in the forest.

Ruby waved a hand.

Slate watched, dazed, as his loincloth appeared around his hips. Then as her dress of shadows wrapped around her skin, a flash of her dagger on her thigh before the dress's long folds covered it.

Slate stared as a slow realization washed over him. Whatever they had done, it had turned Ruby into something... *else*. Her chin was high as ever, but it was less defiant and more assured. Like she knew nothing in this forest could hurt her. Her skin shone with sweat, but there was nothing weary in her posture. She looked like she could take on a god.

Then she breathed out a long sigh, and she was his witch again.

"Okay," Ruby said breathily. She wobbled, and Slate moved automatically to steady her.

She leaned against him with a grateful smile.

"Thank you," she said. "This is... an adjustment. Could you do something else for me?"

"Anything," Slate vowed.

Ruby smiled and pressed a kiss to his palm.

"Open a portal to Sweetsguard," she said. "And fast. They don't have much time."

NINETEEN

One moment, Ruby's mind was full of nothing but pleasure.

Then the ward started glowing, and she was filled with so much *more*.

She was still reeling when she stumbled through the portal, and Slate held her arm to make sure she didn't fall over.

"Ruby," he said. "What *happened*?"

Ruby giggled. She couldn't help it. She also couldn't help the shudder that ran through her as another burst of magic jolted her, filling her with a power she had never even dreamed of when she was the guardian witch of Sweetsguard.

"I'll tell you later," she said, only slurring a little. "Come on."

She tugged him toward the trees. Her hometown was not far, and the screaming was starting.

Slate's ears twitched as the first horrified yell rang through the trees. "What is that?"

"You'll see in a second." She tugged harder. Then she stopped, her bleary brain reminding her of something she had forgotten among all the fizzing magic and ritualistic fucking.

"Slate," she said. "You should—"

Slate scooped her up in his arms before she even had the chance to say it. Ruby clung to his neck and giggled as he started to sprint. She could feel magic in her fingers and come dripping down her thighs, and she had a sneaking suspicion that everything was going to be okay.

After the screaming ended, anyway.

They burst out of the woods to find the small town of Sweetsguard awash with shade demons.

Slate growled. He glared up at the shades swooping down to claw the cowering townsfolk, yanking on the barred bakery door and trashing the broken Paimon ward in the middle of the town square.

"They're not all yours," Ruby assured him. "They teamed up with others outside the ward limits. Can you—?"

She didn't get the chance to finish her sentence. He had already set her down and taken off sprinting toward the nearest demon.

Ruby watched with barely concealed glee as he jumped mightily into the air and grabbed a demon around the ankle. He brought the demon down with a roar, slamming it onto the ground with such force the cobblestones cracked.

Ruby laughed. Then she noticed how many people were shrieking and fleeing for their lives and collected herself.

She ran into the town square and raised her arms.

"I will give you one last chance to retreat," she called.

Not a single demon looked her way. But several townsfolk did, their expressions twisting in terror as they noticed her flowing black gown.

"Glenda told the truth," one woman yelled from her hiding spot beneath an overturned milk cart. "It is the witch, transformed to her true form and returning to kill us all!"

Ruby sighed.

Slate bounded to her side, his claws wet with demon blood. He gave her a look that was both confused and searching. She knew it in her bones: he was with her whatever she decided to do next.

She wanted to kiss the demon blood off his mouth. She settled for turning back to the sky, still thick with demons, and gritting her teeth. Magic crackled up her arms, her irises glinting dark blue.

"I will take out as many as I can," she said, her voice splintering into something twisted and thick. "You deal with the rest."

Slate's black eyes widened as he saw the magic sparking around her. Then he set his jaw and nodded.

Ruby grinned. The more magic that swelled around her, the more demons took notice. Some of them were slowing or even stopping in midair, pointing for the others to watch the strange little witch who had started glowing.

Ruby snarled a word that had been dead for a hundred mortal generations and threw the roiling jets of magic as hard as she could. A dozen screamed out and fell from the sky, holes burning through their torsos.

Slate growled and took off, launching himself at a demon who had stopped clawing through a door to gawk. He plunged his claws through the demon's chest and threw him into another demon, both of them going down in a crunching pile of ash.

Demonic cries of outrage poured from all sides of town. Demons rushed into the square, most of them aiming for Ruby.

Ruby raised her hands again. They were shaking, but it was hard to care with so much magic pouring through her. She could feel it fizzing in her bones, burning through her blood. Dark and horrifying and beautiful, just like the monster she had bound herself to.

"LEAVE US OR DIE," she yelled, throwing another whipcord of magic.

Demons slammed out of the sky, caught by the speeding chord. Others dodged it, still aiming for her.

Slate caught them one by one. He bit off their heads or shredded their chests with his claws, grabbing them with his tail and dragging them in to be slaughtered.

Not a single demon made it to Ruby, who stood in the middle of the blasted town square and shot down every demon foolish enough to try and take her down. By the time the town fell silent, Ruby and Slate stood in the middle of a hundred ashy demon corpses as they watched the few smart demons fly away to safety.

One last demon made a weak swipe at Ruby's ankle.

Ruby stabbed it through the hand. Slate stood on its head, grinding it to dust.

Slate turned to Ruby. "Are you alright?"

Ruby wiped her dagger on her dress and slid it back into its holster band. "I'm fine. You?"

"They barely touched me." Slate gathered her face in his bloody hands, his thumbs rubbing gore into her cheeks.

For a moment Ruby felt like there was no one else in the world. She wanted to melt into him, to have him take her right there in the middle of town square on top of all the corpses they'd made together.

Then a timid throat cleared, and Ruby remembered there were still people watching.

She turned. The bakery door creaked open, towns-folk peeking out from behind the makeshift barricade they'd erected when the demons started attacking. Either they had gotten lucky, or they'd started running demon drills after all, like Ruby always told them to.

Glenda stood at the front of the crowd, trembling limb to limb. She tried to turn around, but someone behind her shoved her back.

Glenda cursed her quietly and turned to face Ruby. "We... we thank you for saving us, O witch."

Slate snorted. He gave Ruby a questioning look, and

Ruby knew he was asking if she would like him to kill this woman.

She shook her head. Glenda was annoying but not dangerous.

"She deserves more than your thanks," Slate said darkly. "I would have let you die in a second. *She* saved you. You should be on your knees in worship."

Glenda's knees hit the damaged cobblestones. She wasn't the only one—everyone who was in sight dropped to their knees, some of them in sheer terror and others in reverent admiration. The latter shook Ruby more than the first; fear and distrust, she was used to. She had no idea what to do with all that admiration.

"We will do whatever you wish," Glenda babbled. "The Bygone is right; we would be dead without you. You don't think you could..."

Her panicked gaze darted toward the broken ward in the middle of the square.

Ruby sighed and stepped up to it. It was riddled with cracks, stone crumbling into the cobblestones below. The ward rune was unrecognizable.

"I will renew your ward," she said. "But first, I should explain how things are going to work from here on."

Glenda nodded, dazed. She bent down and dropped her head onto the cobblestones. "Whatever you say, my lady!"

Slate stepped up beside her again. He gave her another questioning look, and the wonder in his eyes made her want to kiss him all over again.

She resisted the urge, turning back to the townsfolk.

"So," she said. "To begin—"

A friendly bark cut her off.

Ruby tried to hold back a smile. "I'm sorry. Were *you* saying something?"

All eyes turned to the dog spirit, who trotted up to Ruby and sat down heavily on top of a dead demon.

Slate frowned. "Dog. What are you doing here? What happened to your head?"

The spirit looked up at the goat horns that had sprouted from its skull.

"I will give you two guesses, old friend," said the dog spirit formerly known as Paimon, in a voice that Ruby sometimes heard in dreams. "And the first one doesn't count."

Slate rocked back in surprise. Then he sighed. "I should have known. Nobody else is that annoying."

The dog spirit chuckled. There was a short bleat somewhere in the middle and a growl at the end.

"Apologies," he said. "I have been so many things by now. I sometimes get them confused. Ruby, maybe you *should* be the one to explain."

"I would be happy to," Ruby said.

She took Slate's dripping hand. Then she turned to the gaping townsfolk. Some of them had obviously caught onto what was happening since they started clasping their hands together and praying in shocked whispers that echoed over the square while everyone else looked around in confusion.

"Our goat deity, Paimon," she began, letting the

oblivious ones gasp in realization. "Tired of his godly existence. He had been human, and then a god, and now he wanted to experience something new."

"Something carefree," the dog spirit interjected, tail thumping happily. "Something small and simple. Hence: dog spirit!"

"Good choice," Slate said faintly. "You might have told me, old friend."

"I tried. You would not wake until after I made the change." The dog spirit licked Slate's bloody hand. "It is good to see you awake."

Then the dog spirit turned to Ruby, its gaze light and unbothered. "Ruby! Thank you for taking my power from the ward. I think I still have some to spare. Would you like it?"

Ruby considered. She *did* like this power. It lit her up in ways she didn't know were possible. But if she accepted the full power of a god, she would lose things in return. She liked her humanity. She wanted some of it to stay, at the very least.

"Not yet," she decided.

The dog spirit bowed his head. "As you wish. I will see you back in the void. Mortals, goodbye!"

Several townsfolk stuttered a stunned goodbye, including several of Glenda's children who looked delighted to see a talking dog, never mind that he was the former god of the town.

The dog spirit vanished.

Slate pulled Ruby's hand, turning her away from the whispering townsfolk. His eyes were huge and confused behind his skull mask, staring at her in a way that made her anxious. The confidence of a god was starting to dim, leaving her with her usual human nerves once more.

Ruby wiped a smear of blood off her neckline. "What? Do I look okay?"

"You look..." Slate's brow furrowed behind the mask. "Resplendent. Ruby, I... What *are* you?"

Ruby laughed, short and wild. "I don't know! I'm not a human. I'm not a god. Not all the way, anyhow. I'm... whatever I want to be. Within limits."

Slate didn't respond. His hand clenched around hers, a strange look entering his dark eyes. It looked a lot like hope.

"Witch god," a voice called from the back of the bakery. "There are wings on the horizon!"

Ruby looked up and sighed. More demons were heading their way, barely specks in the distance.

"One second," she told Slate.

She turned toward the ruined ward and held out her hands. She could still feel the power they created during the ritual and Slate's come dripping down her thighs.

Magic crackled at her fingertips. Her hole throbbed with it, pulsing in time with her heartbeat. She still ached from taking his cock, and she was deeply glad for it.

She touched the ward stone. It glowed blue under her touch, light springing out and filling a nearby crack. That light bled into the next one, and soon, all the cracks were glowing with light, the townsfolk covering their eyes as it swelled.

Ruby stepped back.

The light died. A new ward stone sat in the middle of town, shiny and perfect. The rune was different: instead of goat horns, there sat a crude, slim dagger.

There was a faint shriek in the distance. Ruby smiled and looked up to see the demons falling out of the sky, writhing.

The ward was renewed. The town of Sweetsguard was safe again.

A lone cheer rang through the square.

"The demons are banished," cried Glenda, grabbing her children away from their impassioned whispers about the see-through dog to hug them close. "Praise our new god witch, Ruby!"

"Oh, I don't think that's necessary," Ruby began.

But it was too late. The townsfolk were crowding out of the bakery, popping out of overturned wagons, and running from their houses to rejoice at their savior. Many of them stumbled to a stop when they noticed Slate lingering behind her but calmed once they saw everyone in the bakery cheering.

Then the questions started.

"What do you wish to be called, god witch?"

"Would you like sacrifices, god witch?"

"How is the Bygone involved? Should we pray to him, too?"

Ruby backed away, bewildered by all the clamoring and kneeling and people trying to thrust flowers and gold into her hands.

She turned to Slate, only to find him walking toward the forest.

"Hold that thought," she told the people bustling to get their question asked first.

She ran to Slate and ducked in front of him. "Where are you going?"

"Home. To the void." Slate gave her a tight smile. It did not reach his eyes. "You will want to address your new followers. At least, they appreciate you now."

"*Followers*?" Ruby laughed. "Slate—"

But Slate was gone. Ruby touched the shadows swirling in the air where he had been standing and sighed. She had recognized the anguish in his eyes. The same look had been in her eyes an hour ago.

"You idiot Skullstalker," she whispered.

She turned to address the waiting crowd. First, she would talk to her old town. Then she would return to the void.

Her void. If she was lucky.

TWENTY

late stared down at his forest nest, his fists clenched.

His claws dug into his skin. He ignored them. What was a little more blood? He would clean himself up later, but for now, he wanted...

He *wanted*...

Slate growled, stalking around his nest angrily. He *wanted* his witch. But failing that, he wanted to collapse into his nest and sleep for a hundred years. He could even do that without risking Ruby dying while he slept, now that she was a god.

Half-god. Whatever Ruby was, she would last more than a puny eighty years. And she would have a wonderful time in that squalid little town, where the people finally treated her like she deserved.

He reared his fist back, about to punch through a tree.

Then he paused.

Something had changed since he had appeared in his realm. He had been so busy grinding his fangs about Ruby that he hadn't noticed what it was. Now it was finally setting in.

"Would you look at that," came a familiar voice. "It's dark! I thought it would be evening for the next century, at least."

"It was dark before," Slate replied. He turned grudgingly to see Paimon, or at least, the simplified shadow of him, sitting on a nearby rock.

The dog spirit jumped down, tail wagging lazily. "It was *almost* dark. Now it is *properly* dark. Night has fallen in the Bygone void once again."

"I don't even know where that stupid name came from," Slate said bitterly.

The dog spirit let out a knowing rumble. "You slept for many generations. Mortals make up all sorts of stories."

He leaped up on Slate's nest, ignoring his glare.

"I must say," the dog spirit continued, pawing at the shredded fur lining the nest. "That worked out better than I intended. Now if you don't mind, I will go back to simply being a dog spirit now."

Slate thought about arguing. But he had never been able to talk Paimon out of anything. If the old goat's mind was made up, that was the end of that.

"Do whatever you wish," he said quietly.

The dog spirit laid his head on his paws. "Goodbye, old friend. I had such fun."

Between one blink and the next, something crucial

sparked out of its eyes. The dog spirit snuggled further into the nest, utterly content.

Slate watched the spirit angrily. He wanted to howl, to run through the woods until he couldn't feel his legs. He wanted to talk to his friend, but everyone was gone from him now.

He sat down resentfully in the nest next to the snoring dog spirit. Then he curled up, thinking of the dress Ruby had left behind.

He would find it for his nest. He needed something to remember her by, even if it would inevitably lose her scent.

Slate looked up at the never-ending forest. He had been alone for a long time, but he had never been so lonely until that moment.

A loud rip made him startle. His claws shot out and he rose, only to stare as he watched a familiar shadow-clad leg appear through a glowing portal.

"Still not as easy as it should be," Ruby Waterstone announced as she emerged into his void.

The dog spirit stood, shaking its head in annoyance at the loud noise.

"Hello, Dog," Ruby said as it trotted into the forest. She ran her finger down the middle of the portal and watched it seal up. Then she paused, looking up at the sky.

"Would you look at that," she said, marveling. "It's dark."

"Ruby," Slate breathed.

Ruby turned to face him. She was still so small, even

as half a god. He wanted to crush her close and never let her leave.

But he would. The knowledge was like rot on his tongue, but he would do it. For her.

"What are you doing here?" he asked quietly.

Ruby gave him a smile that was so sad his heart clenched. "Can I not visit my lovely Bygone?"

Slate frowned. Was she really joking at a time like this?

Ruby's smile dimmed. She stepped closer, her dress sweeping over the shadowy leaves. She looked like she was a part of the void, a thought so potent it threatened to swallow Slate whole.

"My Bygone," she repeated. "My Slate. You... fulfilled your half of the binding. What will you have of me?"

Make her stay! It rioted inside him, even with all his determination that he would never.

"I would have you..." He ground his fangs until his gums stung. The words were on the tip of his tongue. He had to force them back.

"I would have you live the life you wish," he spat. "I hope your townsfolk continue to treat you as you deserve."

Ruby blinked. Her eyelashes were longer, he realized. Longer and darker, more spiderweb than lash now.

"Sweetsguard," she said. "You think I'm returning to Sweetsguard?"

The question made his heart leap. But Slate didn't let himself hope yet.

"That was always your plan," he said. "And you always wanted them to like you. Now they do."

"They *worship* me." Ruby rolled her eyes. "I never wanted worship. At least, not like that."

She stepped ever closer. Her dress brushed his foot, and Slate stopped breathing.

"I did want them to like me," she admitted. "Now I want something more."

Slate's claws twitched to grab her and hold her close. He resisted.

"A void?" he rasped. "Something fit for a god?"

She laughed again, brighter than anything he'd ever heard in his dark void.

"No," she said. "You."

She reached up and stroked his skull mask. Her thumb trailed along the seam where bone met skin, and Slate couldn't hold back anymore.

He picked her up and dragged her into a kiss, his claws twisting in her hair.

"You want to stay with me?" he asked, panting as they tore apart.

Ruby nodded wildly. "I'll still visit Sweetsguard, keep it safe. But I want to live here. With you. If you'll have me."

She bit her lip. She even had the audacity to look shy.

Slate kissed her again until that shyness was replaced by an endearing giggle. Then he dropped to his knees in the leaves, holding her up above him.

"Until our souls dissolve to dust," he vowed. "I will have you, my little witch. My sweet, beloved mortal."

"Not so mortal anymore," she whispered.

She stroked his horns, his skull mark, his pointed fangs. Things she had been so scared of at the beginning, convinced he would devour her whole.

He still planned to. Just not in the way she feared.

He was about to pull her into another kiss when light streamed past Ruby's head. Slate squinted, temporarily convinced that she was ascending to a second godhood.

Ruby twisted. Orange light streaked over her raven hair, making it glow.

"It's morning," she gasped.

Slate craned his head. Dawn was rising in his void for the first time in an age.

Ruby turned back to him, grinning. Her hand grazed his loincloth, dipping under the dark fabric.

"How long until that ward needs renewing?" she asked.

Slate groaned as she touched his tender knot.

"A long time," he told her and rolled over to press her into the dirt. "But we can practice."

Eighty Years Later

Slate woke as he often did.

With his wife's mouth around his cock.

Slate growled, his hand sliding into Ruby's long, soft hair. She was lying beside him in their nest, her hips grinding into the layers of furs lining the castle walls.

"My little witch," Slate rumbled. He stroked her scalp fondly. Her mouth was stretched unnaturally wide around him, her throat bulging around his shaft.

Slate lay a finger on her neck, feeling his cock twitch inside her when she swallowed. Ruby made sure to take full, frequent advantage of the enchantment Slate had sought out all those years ago to allow her body to adapt to his impossible girth. There was rarely a day that passed where she did not take his cock in some way.

Slate's head fell back against the nest, morning light streaming through the castle window. Time had been mirroring the mortal realm for many years now to Ruby's continued delight.

Slate brushed the hair out of her face. He did not care about the passage of time the same way his wife did, but he did enjoy seeing her bare form in the sunlight.

"You feel perfect," he told her, watching her mouth bob up and down on his cock. "Will I come down your throat? Or is there another hole you want me to fill?"

Ruby pulled off, her mouth red and puffy. For a moment, she did nothing but pant, and Slate brushed a claw over her cheek, marveling at her beauty. She had changed slightly since he first met her, but only what she allowed: wrinkles at the corners of her eyes, lines of grey in her hair. She was thinking about letting the grey take over more. Slate didn't mind. She could look as old as she wanted, as long as her god powers kept her young inside.

Ruby pressed a kiss to the end of his cock. "You decide today, my love."

Slate rumbled contentedly and sat up, throwing her down onto the nest.

Ruby beamed up at him, her dark eyes glowing with excitement. Still just as eager as she was the first time that she took all of him.

Slate surged down and kissed her so long and deep he left dents on her cheek when he pulled back. Ruby could make herself invulnerable if she wanted, or at least enough to not worry about his skull mask leaving marks. But she preferred not to.

I like it when you mark me, she said to him often. Usually when he was kissing those marks away or laving his tongue over them until they faded.

He pressed inside her slowly. He still loved feeling her stretch around him, her walls fluttering as her insides moved to accommodate him.

She placed her hands on her stomach, waiting. "*Gods.* Come on, do it."

"Patience," he told her. He forced himself to hold back, to keep his hips slow and careful until his knot brushed her entrance.

Ruby groaned. Her stomach was bulging under her hands. She rubbed his cockhead through her skin. He could hardly feel it, but the idea was—as always—enough to make him moan and fuck into her properly.

The room filled with the slick, desperate sounds of mating. Slate gathered her hands and pressed them into the nest above her head, watching how they pushed so deep into the lush fur they were almost hidden from view.

"My little beauty," he groaned into her skin. He sped up, basking in her cries. "My sweet, stubborn witch. You take me so well, every time."

Ruby groaned. She was often beyond speech when he fucked her this fast, her mouth hanging open and wordless as she gazed up at him.

"*Slate*," she managed.

She dragged him down into a kiss. He curled over her, pressing his tongue down her throat and fucking her from both holes until she spasmed and cried out around him, muffled.

He withdrew his tongue and ran it down her body,

fondling her breasts. She was clenching down around him, her breathing hitching with amazed sobs as if she still couldn't believe it was this good, even after so many times.

Slate grabbed her hair, pulling her face up. "Say it."

"*Yours*," she whimpered.

Slate shuddered and came. He pulsed deep inside—once, twice, making her stomach bulge even further—before pulling out and finishing over her deflating stomach.

Ruby was still panting as he finished, sagging over her.

She made a sleepy noise against his chest. "Want your knot."

"You want this, too." He rubbed his come against her hip, watching it slide into the nest below.

She grunted. "Both."

"I will knot you tonight." He kissed the dent his skull mask had left on her cheek and sat up. "Breakfast? We have that sausage you like."

Ruby hummed. Something dark gleamed in her eyes, dark and fond and not entirely mortal.

"Later," she said. She hooked a finger around the edge of his skull mask and pulled.

But before Slate could let himself be dragged back down, something throbbed in the back of his head.

He gently caught her wrist. "We have a visitor."

Ruby fell back against the nest with a sigh. "When you said you were getting more attuned, I was so excited for you. I didn't realize it would cut into so much of our time."

Slate snorted, amused. "So much of our time? The last soul to turn up here came months ago."

"We keep each other *very* busy," Ruby purred. She shot him a gleeful grin and stood, shadows wrapping around her skin until she was wearing the same sleek dress he had crafted for her that first week. She had made some alterations, but the shape remained the same: a black, flowing dress with a plunging neckline and a slit up the side.

Ruby posed, her leg slipping out the slit. "Well? Are you going to lie there all day or are you coming with me?"

Slate had spent so long in his nest over the millennia. He was never so happy to be pulled out of it until Ruby arrived.

The lost soul was wandering at the edge of the forest. It wasn't dead, which was a relief. Ruby got sad if they had too many dead wanderers in a row.

The nymph was terrified, staring around the shadowy trees with abject terror. Slate assumed it had never seen a tree like that before, despite being a tree spirit. Nymphs tended to live in pretty, fresh trees, not the void ones dripping shadow.

"Hello," Slate called, making sure his voice was less snarly than usual.

The nymph shrieked. It sounded like a branch snapping. Then it whirled, and Slate's heart softened as it saw the new blossoms growing over the nymph's cheeks. This was a youngling, separated from its colony possibly for the first time.

"I will not harm you," Slate assured it. "I am a guide. Where were you before?"

The nymph trembled. Slate was reminded how much easier dead ones were—often, they were too out of it to be terrified of him.

Then the nymph paused. It had noticed Ruby standing next to him, waving sweetly.

"Hello," Ruby called. "Good to see you! Welcome to the wanderer's void. Would you mind telling my husband where you were before this, so he can return you there?"

The nymph uncurled from its horrified slouch. Its blossoms opened curiously, and it took a hesitant step toward them.

"That's what I said," Slate muttered, annoyed.

Ruby patted his hip. "It's the way you say it, dear."

The nymph rubbed the moss on its arms, leaves sprouting from between its fingers.

"I-I was walking behind my family," it began. "They told me to stay close, but I didn't listen. There was a beautiful crystal flower bush, and I only wanted to look at it!"

"Crystal flower," Ruby said. "Was this in the Crystal Wastes?"

The nymph nodded. Ruby gave him a significant

look. Crystal Wastes were one of the many, *many* places in the mortal realm where the veil was thin. Ruby knew them as well as he did, nowadays. Possibly even better. She knew much more about the mortal realm.

Slate concentrated, his eyes glowing behind his mask as he read the nymph's heart.

The connection was strong. He could read all the confusion and fear inside it, the longing for its family, for their comforting branches to wrap around its thin, spiky form.

Slate bowed his head. "I send you back, young one."

The nymph's eyes bloomed wide.

Its mouth opened. "Thank—"

Then it was gone. A single rose petal drifted where it stood, swept up by a warm breeze.

Ruby wound a shred of shadow around her finger and leaned on Slate's arm. "Did it get home safe?"

Slate focused, pulling the connection he had kept in a loose grip. He could see the crystal-lined path, the nymph's bewildered relief turning to joy as it spotted its family. He got the briefest impression of branches wrapping the nymph close before the connection dissolved, leaving Slate with a warm feeling of home that didn't fade as he returned to himself.

"It got home," he confirmed. "It is with its family now."

Ruby hummed happily. The shadowy leaves around her gusted up in a happy torrent, and Slate watched them with contentment he hadn't known was possible until a mortal stumbled into his void and bound him.

"That's enough work for today, I think," Ruby said. She tapped his arms, and Slate lifted her obediently until she could kiss him without straining.

Ruby brushed their noses together. "Take me back to bed."

Slate growled, walking them back until she was pressed into a tree.

"Why?" he asked, voice low. "Are you still sleepy?"

Ruby giggled. "No. But I want you inside me again at least once before you make me breakfast."

"As my witch requests," Slate said, starting the trek back to the castle.

Ruby slid her hand under his loincloth, halting his gait.

"No," she said, her mouth brushing his jaw. "Here. Now."

Slate groaned, stiffening under her touch. He ran a hand down her dress, the shadowy material dissipating until she was naked in his arms.

"Good," Ruby whispered. "Now, take me, my beloved Bygone."

Slate growled and did.

Much later, Slate crawled back into his nest with his wife in his arms.

She settled against him, sweaty and satisfied. She fell asleep as soon as her head hit his chest, snoring softly.

Slate stared at the castle ceiling, waiting. He slept less often these days, though he was still difficult to wake up.

Slate stroked her hair and curled tighter around Ruby's sleeping body. He could feel sleep rising to claim him.

His eyes drifted shut. If he did oversleep, his wife would be there to wake him.

EPILOGUE

This bonus epilogue is a stretch goal unlocked by the lovely backers of the BOUND Kickstarter campaign!

Ruby watched the portal flicker, impatient.

"It's been more than two minutes," she called.

She wasn't expecting a response. Slate couldn't hear her through the jagged tear between their void and the mortal realm. If she squinted, she could see the black depths of Anderfel, the patch of mortal realm where Slate's mysterious brother resided.

Ruby sighed. At least, it was a lovely summer day in their void. The forest was still dripping shadows, but they didn't touch the clearing she was standing in. It was one of many clearings that had cropped up in this void since Ruby made it her home. The forest was no longer just dirt and trees, but *grass*. Green and fresh and warm from the sun.

Ruby flexed her bare toes in the springy grass a moment longer before she gave in and marched toward the portal.

Then she froze. There was something huge and dark approaching from the other side. Something dangerous. Something that sparked fear into countless mortals and demons alike.

Ruby beamed as her husband stepped into the clearing. "Slate! You took your time."

"I was several minutes, as discussed," Slate replied. He was carrying a large golden bowl filled with herbs. Some of them were whole, some crushed, and some ground into a dark green paste that pooled at the very bottom of the bowl.

"Two," Ruby corrected, eyeing the bowl curiously. "You said *two*. Where's your brother?"

She peered behind him into the portal. Slate ran a claw over the rip in space, and it healed over.

"He is not coming," Slate said as the portal closed. "He has given us all we need to perform the ritual ourselves. And knowing now what must be done, I am glad for it."

Ruby giggled. She had laughed so little in her mortal days, which were a fuzzy memory after all these generations spent as the half-god she had become.

"Oh?" Ruby said, stroking her husband's bare chest. "And what must be done, my dear?"

Slate smiled, small and fanged. He took one hand off his bowl to run a gentle claw over her laugh lines, which had been getting deeper despite her magic.

Half-gods only lasted so long. Centuries, but not millennia. They had known for decades that they would need a spell. And now they finally had it.

Ruby picked up an herb from the bowl Slate was holding. "I don't recognize any of this. I was an expert in mortal herbs, once."

"In your country," Slate reminded her. "Many strange plants grow in Anderfel. But I will admit that some of them seem to come from somewhere else entirely."

Ruby rubbed the herb between her fingers, watching it crumble. "And we're sure it will work?"

"We are," Slate agreed. His claw drifted down her face and over her neck until it rested on the edge of her dress. "Would you like to know what must happen?"

"I would."

"Good," Slate said quietly.

He slid his claw down her dress. The shadows parted easily under his touch, until the dress was gone and Ruby stood naked in the clearing. Once, she would have shivered. But sunlight was a frequent visitor to Slate's void now, the light intensifying as soon as Ruby bared her skin. Attuned, as always, to the creatures who resided inside it.

"Sounds like my kind of ritual," Ruby said breathlessly. She reached for Slate's loincloth, only to have him bat her hand away.

"I will join you in a moment," he assured her. Then he began walking around her, sprinkling the strange herbs in a huge circle. The fresh grass bristled underneath it, emanating a dark light that reminded Ruby of Slate's glowing eyes.

Ruby pointed toward the bowl. "Can I help? I used to do this for a living, you know."

"My brother prepared most of it while I was there," Slate replied. He stepped into the glowing circle he had made out of the herbs and scooped the dark green paste out of the bowl. But instead of applying it to Ruby's naked body, like she expected, Slate rubbed a circle around his own heart.

Ruby blinked, charmed. It made sense, of course—the spell would bind her to his lifespan, after all. Of course, he would be a key element.

After carefully meeting the ends of the circle, Slate dipped his fingers back into the bowl and lifted them toward Ruby.

Ruby stroked her long, dark hair out of the way. Sure enough, Slate drew a circle around her heart. The paste was cool and smelled of spices she didn't recognize. It made her wonder if they should travel more of the mortal realm. But that usually caused more trouble than it was worth, especially when they strayed outside of Ruby's well-trod domain of Sweetsguard.

Slate set the bowl on the grass, outside the circle. "How do you wish to do this?"

Ruby thought about it. "Lie down."

Slate huffed but did. The circle around him pulsed

with light, tendrils sneaking out to curl around his horns. The dark threads that wavered around Slate's skull mask climbed up to meet them, light and dark shifting curiously around each other.

Ruby admired the strands for a moment. Then she climbed on top of her husband, spreading her legs wide around his large thighs.

"I want you to look at me like you worship me," Ruby said as she took his hardening cock in her hand and guided him toward her hole.

Slate's glowing eyes flared. "That will not be difficult. I worship you daily. The spell will only assist with this."

"Oh?" Ruby bit her lip as she guided him inside, sinking down in a way no mortal could accommodate. "H-how so?"

Slate growled. He gripped her legs, his claws digging into them in a way that would have once torn her flesh. Now they only left dents, and that was purely because they both enjoyed them.

"*Join our lifelines*," Slate began as she continued to sink slowly onto his length.

There was an inhuman hiss under his voice. *Even less human than normal*, Ruby corrected herself with a fond smile. His eyes gleamed brighter than ever, the color identical to the circle emanating around them.

"*My bride will not fade*," Slate continued, breath growing ragged as Ruby continued rocking down onto him. "*Nor wither, nor rot. She will bind eternally to my life.*"

His voice echoed around the clearing, grass rustling

with its force. If Ruby were mortal, it would have hurt her ears. But it only ached, as pleasant as the claw marks he left in her skin.

Ruby came to a stop, his cock as deep as it would go. Which, thanks to the magic spell he cast on himself all those years ago, was every inhuman inch of him, Ruby's stomach bulging unnaturally with it.

They both groaned as Ruby rubbed his cock through her stomach. He couldn't feel it, he told her once, but that wasn't the point. The point was how *full* she looked.

The circle glowed brighter. Ruby started to ride Slate, her breath hitching as she pushed herself up on her knees.

"Slate," she said. "The spell."

Slate blinked, his grip sinking tighter around her thighs. The dark strands of shadow around his skull mask latched onto the tendrils of light from the circle glowing around them.

Connecting them, Ruby realized. Then she noticed a strange tingling sensation and looked down to see the circle on her chest glowing. Slate's circle was glowing too, presumably feeding him the same odd, vibrating sensation that was slowly filling Ruby to the brim.

"*I bind you to me*," Slate said, his voice barely audible through the growling. "*To my life. My soul. You will exist until I am no more. Do you accept?*"

Ruby grinned. There was no offer for him to reject the binding she cast on him the first time she met. But he had made sure there was a chance now. It was probably why the meeting with his brother took so long—he was figuring out how to make the spell end in a question rather than a command.

"Yes," Ruby gasped.

The circles smudged into their chests burst into light. The tingling sensation in her chest exploded through the rest of her body, filling her with such pleasure that she jerked to a stop, and they both shouted as it surged through them.

The light swelled. Ruby didn't need to close her eyes, keeping them open to stare at her lovely, monstrous husband as the spell radiated through the clearing. Light swirled around them, rustling the grass and swirling the shadowy trees, but Ruby barely noticed. She couldn't take her eyes off Slate, who was staring up at her in amazement.

In all her time as a half-god, Ruby had never felt more holy.

Finally, the light dissipated. The tingling sensation went with it, leaving them both panting and shaking against each other.

Slate ran a trembling hand up her back. He was soft inside her, his knot fat and full in her hole. Apparently, he had come during the spell's climax. Ruby couldn't blame him; she wasn't sure her legs could hold her up if she tried to stand.

"You bound me," Ruby murmured against his chest.

Slate chuckled, a rumbling noise that was once so rare, nobody alive remembered it.

"You bound me first," he reminded her.

Ruby rubbed her cheek against his cool skin, rocking

gently to enjoy the tug of the knot buried deep inside her. "How long do you think you have left?"

"A few millennia," Slate replied.

"Do you think that's enough?"

Slate wrapped her in his arms. His dark eyes burned into hers, and Ruby couldn't see how she could have ever feared him. Her sweet monster, sleeping away the centuries until his wife showed up.

"Enough time to love you?" Slate asked. "Never. But it will have to do."

Special Thanks

Thank you so much for reading Bound, the first book in the Skullstalker Brides series! You can get the second book, Held, on Amazon, B&N or KU.

If you want to support me, please leave a review on Goodreads, Amazon and any social media of your choice.

Acknowledgments

Firstly, let's hear it for the amazing Kickstarter backers who brought this book to life:

Effy, Megan I, Heather D, Elisha Padilla, Amanda McColly, Makinley Karnivorous, Molly Fessel, Wren Jones, Alaina, Nora, Ashley Bradley, Anonymous, Mistress Sharon, Elizabeth Murphy, Juliana Chiari, Kat Simmons, Christina Getzen, thebiblioaddict, Hailey, Lexi, Iesha Parker-Gask, Raven Friday, Anonymous, Mari T, Daytona M, Kirsty E, Simone Sexton, Megan Long, Nery M Silva, Desiree Montoya-Reeb, Kayla, Zoldos, Amanda Hobbs, Chelsea L, Shelli, Arthur Wilson, Minnie!, Amanda Gauthier, Mandi Corman-Draper, Kaprice Rowe, Shavon Bledsoe, Axel KNG, Katie Yoes, Lexie K, Donna, Stephen B, Dragonskull817.

And now let's hear it for the publishing team! Edward Giordano, formatter extraordinaire, my fabulous editor Naomi Darling, my cover artist Rana Dela (ranadela_x on Instagram), And last but not least, my fantastic beta reader, Matthew (Dragon68).

About the Author

Isabelle Taylor writes sweet, steamy fantasy romance. She works in a bookstore in New Zealand and has a Creative Writing Masters from the International Institute of Modern Letters.

She can be found on Instagram and TikTok @isabelletaylorauthor.

instagram.com/isabelletaylorauthor

tiktok.com/@isabelletaylorauthor

9 781067 061722